WINIFRED FINLAY

Tales from the Borders

Illustrated by Victor Ambrus

KAYE & WARD
LONDON

First published by Kaye & Ward Ltd,
21 New Street, London EC2M 4NT
1979

ISBN 0 7182 1225 8

Set in VIP Palatino by S. G. Mason (Chester) Ltd.
Printed in Great Britain at The Fakenham Press Ltd.

Contents

The Waters of Life   1

The Red Bull of Norroway   15

Killmoulis   24

The Milkmaid of Whittingham   38

The Outlandish Knight   50

The King and the Miller of Tweed   60

The Milk-white Doo   69

The Lord's Daughter and the Seal Folk of the Farnes   76

The Laddie who kept Hares   90

The Cowt of Kielder and the Wicked Lord Soulis 101

The Witch of Rubers Law   112

FOR VERITY HARDWICK

The Waters of Life

Once upon a time and a time before that there lived a king who fell so ill that none of the doctors in his kingdom could cure him.

In despair he sent for the Wise Woman from the North, who took one look at him.

"Only the Waters of Life can restore you to health," she said, and turned to go.

"Wait," the king begged. "Tell me where such precious waters can be found."

"In one place only. And that is in a well in the garden of an enchanted castle." She paused.

"Yes, yes," the king cried impatiently. "But where is this enchanted castle?"

"It lies in the middle of a dark sheet of water in the distant and dangerous hills of the Scottish Borderland that lie beyond the bleak and desolate North Countree."

And she hobbled away before more questions could be asked.

"Send for my three sons," the king ordered, and when the princes presented themselves before him, he told them each to take a flask and fasten it to his belt and set off at once to find the Waters of Life in the distant and dangerous hills of the Scottish Borderland that lie beyond the bleak and desolate North Countree.

The three sons took their flasks, mounted their horses, and rode and rode and rode until they came to a crossroads by a stream. Here the way divided into

1

two broad, pleasant paths and one narrow, over-grown track.

The two elder princes took the pleasant paths and fell in with such jovial company that they soon forgot about their father, the king, and the Waters of Life.

As for the youngest prince, he made his way through bramble and briar, marsh and mire, through dense dark forests and swift, swirling rivers until at last, when he was in sight of the bleak and desolate North Countree, he came to a tumbledown cottage in a neglected garden. At the door of the cottage sat an ugly old man.

"So you have come at last," the old man said. "I had almost given up hope of your finding your way here.

"You have a long way to go before you find the Waters of Life, so stable your horse and come in and share my supper."

The youngest prince did as he was bid and ate his share of bread and cheese and drank his share of water.

"There is a bed ready for you in the next room," the old man said when they had finished eating. "Whatever creatures come to share it with you, do not move or utter a sound, for if you do your father will have one son the less in the morning."

Tired out, the prince climbed into the bed and was just going to pull the bedclothes over his head when a crowd of frogs and snails climbed in after him, and the whole night long they jumped and slithered on and around him. Remembering what the old man had said, however, he neither moved nor uttered a sound and, just when he felt he could lie still no longer, a cock crowed once to announce the dawn and immediately the creatures disappeared.

Hoping to snatch a few minutes' sleep, he closed his

eyes, but a moment later the old man knocked loudly on the door and called out that his breakfast was ready.

"Did you sleep well?" he asked, as they ate up the meagre scraps which had been left from the previous night.

"I have slept better but I might have slept worse," the prince replied.

"So it was to be," the old man said, nodding his head.

"There is another horse ready for you at the door. It will take you to my elder brother, who will help you on the next stage of your journey to find the Waters of Life."

When the prince had mounted the horse, the old man gave him a ball of yarn.

"Throw that between the horse's ears," he commanded, and when the prince did so the horse galloped off, almost as swiftly as the wind, until at last as they neared the bleak and desolate North Countree, they came to a tumbledown house in untended grounds. At the door of the house sat a man even older and uglier than the one the prince had left that morning.

"So you have come at last," the old man said. "I suppose my younger brother sent you?"

When the prince agreed that this was so, the old man bade him stable his horse and go in and share his supper.

The prince did as he was bid, ate his share of oatmeal scones and wild brambles and drank his share of ale.

"There is a bed ready for you upstairs," the old man said, when they had finished eating. "Whatever creatures come to share it with you, do not move or utter a sound, for if you do your father will have one son the less in the morning."

Feeling even more tired than on the previous night, the prince climbed into the bed and was just going to pull the bedclothes over his head when a crowd of toads and slow-worms climbed in after him, and the whole night long they jumped and slithered on and around him. Remembering what the old man had said, however, he neither moved nor uttered a sound, and just when he felt he could lie still no longer, a cock crowed twice to announce the dawn and immediately the creatures disappeared.

Hoping desperately to catch a few minutes' sleep, he closed his eyes, but a moment later the old man knocked loudly on the door and called out that his breakfast was ready.

"Did you sleep well?" he asked, as they ate up the meagre scraps which had been left from the previous night.

"I have slept better but I might have slept worse," the prince replied.

"So it was to be," the old man said, nodding his head. "There is another horse ready for you at the door. It will take you to our eldest brother, who will help you on the next stage of your journey to find the Waters of Life."

When the prince had mounted the horse, the old man gave him a ball of yarn.

"Throw that between the horse's ears," he commanded, and when the prince did so the horse galloped off, almost as swiftly as the wind. When at last the bleak and desolate North Countree lay behind them and the dangerous hills of the Scottish Borderland appeared ahead, they came to a ruinous mansion in a vast expanse of waste ground. At the door of the mansion sat the oldest and ugliest man the prince had ever seen.

Again he was invited in, shared the old man's supper of soup made with herbs, and finally went to bed.

This time, however, there was no warning from the old man, and no creatures shared his bed, and so the prince slept soundly until a cock crowed thrice to announce the dawn.

"Did you sleep well?" the old man asked.

"I have never slept better," the prince replied.

"So it was to be," the old man said, nodding his head. "Now listen to me carefully, as there is much for you to do: if you make one mistake your father will have one son the less, while you yourself will be changed into a frog or a snail, a toad or a slow-worm, doomed to live alone among the desolate wastelands of the North Countree.

"Take this ball of yarn and throw it between your horse's ears and then ride so swiftly that the wind cannot see you, until at last you come to the farthermost hills of the dangerous Scottish Borderland. There you will see the enchanted castle surrounded by a sheet of dark water.

"Tether your horse securely to a tree and at the right time call out that you desire to be carried over the water. Three swans will appear and bear you across to the castle, but have a care that you do not slip and fall, for if you do, your father will have one son the less tonight.

"On the far shore you must pass through three gates, each guarded by fearful beasts which sleep an enchanted sleep in the middle of the day, from one until two o'clock.

"Go straight into the castle, past many grand rooms and through the kitchen into the garden. No matter what you may see on the way, do not linger, for you will be safe for only one short hour. In the garden you will find the Well of the Waters of Life. Fill your flask and stopper it securely, and then return the way you came and ride back to me here. But remember this – there is more in your success than affects you or your father."

Thanking the old man, the prince mounted his horse, threw the ball of yarn between its ears and was off so swiftly that the wind could see neither horse nor rider.

All morning he rode until he arrived at the farther-most hills of the Scottish Borderland and there he saw the enchanted castle surrounded by a dark sheet of water. Tethering his horse securely to a tree, he stood on the bank and at the right time he called out that he desired to be carried over the water.

Immediately three white swans appeared and bore him safely across to the castle, and it was exactly one o'clock when he set foot on the far bank.

At the first gate stood two huge giants with spiked clubs in their hands, but now they slept soundly and never moved as the prince passed between them.

At the second gate were two fierce lions with long, sharp teeth, but now they slept soundly and never moved when the prince passed between them.

At the third gate lay two terrible dragons, and though the air was warm from the air they breathed out, now they slept soundly and never moved as the prince passed between them.

Up the steps and into the castle he hurried, passing through many grand rooms, and then suddenly he halted outside the open door of the grandest room of all. There, on a golden bed, spread with gold em-broidered sheets and counterpane, lay the most beautiful princess he had ever seen.

Approaching closer, the prince sighed, because he had fallen in love without knowing it. Closer still the prince approached, and bending down, he kissed the princess.

She did not waken from her enchanted sleep.

Recalling why he was there, he turned to go and suddenly noticed a lace handkerchief on the floor: picking it up he dropped his own in its place – a white handkerchief embroidered in one corner with three golden crowns.

Through the deserted corridors and the empty kitchen he ran, until at last he came to the garden, which was filled with sleeping roses, and there in the centre he saw the Well of the Waters of Life.

Carefully he filled and stoppered his flask and as time was passing so quickly, he ran back through the castle, snatching only the briefest glimpse of the still sleeping princess on the golden bed.

Down the steps he jumped and through the three gates he hurried, past the savage guards still asleep, and once more the three white swans bore him safely over the water.

Just as he set foot on the bank the magic sleeping spell came to an end and a tremendous noise arose from the castle – the blood-curdling cries of angry giants, the fearful snarling of savage lions and the fierce roaring of fire-breathing dragons.

Only the princess did not waken from her enchanted sleep.

Hastily the prince mounted his horse and off they sped through the dangerous hills of the Scottish Borderland, so swiftly that the wind could see neither horse nor rider.

At nightfall, when the Borderland lay behind them

and the North Countree ahead, they arrived at the ruinous mansion of the oldest and ugliest of the three brothers and there the prince dismounted.

"I have helped you," the old man said. "Now it is your turn to help me. Take this sword and walk with me to the well at the back of this mansion and there cut off my head."

"That would be a poor reward for the advice and help you have given me," the prince protested. But the old man insisted so vigorously that at last the prince took the sword, walked to the well, and with one stroke cut off the old man's head.

The moment the head fell into the water, a handsome young man appeared by the prince's side, the ruinous mansion became as splendid as on the day it was built, and the waste ground was transformed into splendid woods and well-kept lawns and gardens.

"I have waited many years for someone brave enough to come and break the spell that was cast on me," the young man said. "Tonight we shall feast together, and afterwards I trust you will serve my younger brothers as you have served me."

Of course the prince was pleased to cut off the head of the second ugly old man, and see him become young and handsome once more and his house and gardens restored to their former conditions.

After they had feasted together he rode on to the first ugly old man, and just as he performed the same service for him, far away the princess in the castle in the Scottish Borderland awoke, stretched her arms and yawned. And at that moment the spell was broken. The giants, lions and dragons vanished, the swans turned into young warriors of noble birth and servants bustled about the castle, which was suddenly linked to the bank by a strong, stone causeway.

The following morning the prince mounted his own horse and rode to the crossroads by the stream where he had arranged to meet his brothers. As they had not yet arrived, he tethered his horse and lay down in the shelter of a tree and, tired after all his adventures and his three nights of feasting and rejoicing, he fell fast asleep.

Presently his two brothers arrived. So concerned had they been with their own pleasure that both had forgotten entirely about the Waters of Life and were only reminded of it by the sight of their sleeping brother.

"I wonder if he found it," the eldest whispered, and removing the flask from the belt of the youngest prince, he tasted the contents and knew the water to be different from any he had ever tasted before and so must indeed be the Waters of Life.

"He is much too young to reap the rewards of such a discovery," the second brother murmured, and he poured half of the Waters of Life into his own flask and half into his elder brother's, and filled up that of the youngest brother from the stream. And off the two of them rode to their father's kingdom.

When the youngest prince awoke he saw by the tracks around him that his brothers had arrived and departed and so off he rode after them; while far away in the castle in the Scottish Borderland the princess picked up the handkerchief embroidered in the corner with three golden crowns and knew that a king's son had visited her during her enchanted sleep.

When at last the youngest prince arrived at his father's palace he was delighted to find him healthy and vigorous again.

"Your brothers spared themselves no trouble or hardship to find and bring back the Waters of Life," the king said in a displeased tone. "However, to be fair, I shall taste the water in your flask too."

At the first mouthful he staggered and almost fell, so sick and weak did he suddenly become.

"You are trying to poison me," he shouted, reaching for one of the other flasks to restore him to health again. "Take my youngest son away," he commanded his executioner, "and cut off his head at once."

And at that moment the princess ordered her horse to be saddled and rode off, calling in turn on the three handsome young men, bidding them put on their shining armour, unsheath their swords and ride with her as her escorts.

The executioner, however, took pity on the youngest prince – whom, indeed, he had always preferred to the elder brothers – and gave him shabby clothes to wear and bade him smear his hands and face with soil; and then he took him secretly to a distant wood where there lived a family of poor charcoal burners. Here the disguised prince was made welcome, and as he worked hard and was always willing to learn, he was soon accepted by the peasants as one of them and shared their simple food, sleeping in the open when it was fine and in a mud hut thatched with branches when it rained.

At last the princess and the three handsome young men in shining armour and with swords drawn reached the palace of the king, and dismounting, they entered and the princess demanded to see the king and his sons.

"I am come to wed that prince who filled his flask from the Well of the Waters of Life in the garden of my castle, which lies in the distant and dangerous hills of the Scottish Borderland," she announced. "Which man was it?"

11

When the eldest prince pushed his way forward eagerly, the princess threw the embroidered handkerchief on the floor.

"Step on that without stumbling," she said.

The eldest prince tried, but no sooner had he put his foot on the handkerchief than he fell and broke his arm.

"You are not the one," the princess said scornfully, whereupon the youngest of the princess's escorts stood guard over him with drawn sword so that he could cause no more trouble.

The second prince had even worse luck. He fell and broke his leg, whereupon the second of the princess's escorts stood guard over him with drawn sword, so that he also could cause no more trouble.

"Have you not another son?" the princess asked.

Now the king trembled and grew pale, knowing he could only send for the executioner and ask what had happened to his youngest son.

"The youngest prince is alive and well and living with a family of charcoal burners in a distant wood," the executioner answered.

"Have him brought to the palace at once," the king commanded, greatly relieved, because he liked neither the look in the princess's eye nor the drawn swords of her escorts.

After some time the messenger returned – alone.

"The prince says he will not come, as he prefers life in the forest to death in the palace."

"Go back and tell him there is no question of death," the king said hastily, considerably frightened by the frown on the princess's face and the drawn swords of her escorts.

Again the messenger returned alone.

"The prince says he still prefers life in the forest, but

you are very welcome to visit him there."

The king did not know whether to be furious at his son's disobedience or terrified at the anger of the princess and her escorts, but before he could say anything more, the princess spoke to the messenger.

"Ask the prince if he is willing to exchange a lace handkerchief for one that he let fall on the floor of the castle in the distant and dangerous hills of the Scottish Borderland."

This time the prince, still in shabby clothes and with dirty hands and face, arrived at the palace before the messenger.

"Can you step on that handkerchief without stumbling?" the princess asked.

And of course the youngest prince could.

And did.

"This is the prince for me," the princess declared, and then she turned to the king. "You are welcome to your two sons. They have deceived you once and I have no doubt will deceive you again."

Now she looked at the two princes who were still lying on the floor with drawn swords above them.

"And you are welcome to your father. He has already ordered the executioner to cut off the head of one son and I have no doubt he will give the same order again before long, and the executioner may not care enough to save your lives."

Finally she turned to the youngest prince.

"Will you come with me and marry me and rule my kingdom?" she asked.

The youngest prince declared that nothing would please him better, and he led the princess out of the palace while the three handsome young men in shining armour followed with drawn swords.

The first thing they did was to go to the wood and

reward the charcoal burners handsomely with money and presents. After that the prince washed and changed into costly garments of silk and velvet, with lace at his neck and wrists – clothes which the princess happened to have brought with her – and then the prince and the princess and the three young men rode off to the castle in the middle of the dark sheet of water in the distant hills of the Scottish Borderland, and their laughter floated back on the wind as a reproach to the dishonest princes and the foolish, bad-tempered king.

The Red Bull of Norroway

Once upon a time there lived in the Lowlands of Scotland a king who had three daughters. The eldest two were vain and selfish and not in the least beautiful, but the youngest was kind and thoughtful and very lovely and her parents cared for her dearly.

Now it happened that one evening the three princesses were talking together and, as so often happens when lassies, rich or poor, are alone, the talk turned to what kind of husbands the future might hold for them.

"I shall marry a king," the eldest princess announced.

"And I a prince – or perhaps I might consider a duke," the second decided.

The youngest princess laughed at her sisters, knowing them to be both proud and conceited.

"I should be quite content to marry the Red Bull of Norroway," she said.

No one thought any more about husbands or weddings that evening, but the next morning there was a terrible roaring and bellowing, a thundering of hoofs and an angry snorting, and when the king opened the door there stood the Red Bull of Norroway, and if there was an uglier beast in the whole of the land, the king had not seen him.

"I have come to claim my bride," roared the Red Bull, and the queen, peering round her husband, grew pale at the thought of giving their kind and lovely daughter to this dreadful creature.

"Let us give him the old henwife instead," she

whispered. "I am quite sure that he will never notice the difference."

And so the old henwife, dressed in the clothes of the youngest princess, was helped onto the back of the Red Bull. Away he charged in a cloud of dust until he came to a magic wood, and the moment he entered it he knew that it was not the youngest princess but the old henwife who was seated on his back. Throwing her angrily to the ground, he returned, roaring and bellowing and demanding his bride, and if he had looked ugly before he looked twice as ugly now.

The king grew as pale as the queen at the thought of giving their kind and lovely daughter to this horrible creature, and so they offered him the maid-servants, one by one, but each time as soon as the Red Bull reached the magic wood he knew it was not the youngest princess seated on his back, and he threw the maidservants down to the ground and returned to the palace.

In despair the king and queen then gave the Bull the eldest princess, and when she was thrown off, the second princess, and finally they knew that there was nothing for it but to help their favourite daughter onto the back of the Red Bull and, weeping bitterly, they watched him charging off in a cloud of dust.

And this time he did not return.

Through the magic wood he galloped and over wide moors and by lonely marshes; up heather-clad hills he climbed and along stony braes until at last he came to a castle where a great company of splendidly dressed people was about to sit down to a feast.

The lord welcomed the two unexpected guests and gave orders for room to be made for them at the table, but just as the princess was about to sit down, she saw a silver pin sticking out of the shoulder of the Red Bull.

Surely such a pin must cause him pain, she thought, and she pulled it out. Immediately the Red Bull disappeared and in his place stood a tall and handsome young prince.

Of course everyone was amazed and delighted, and the princess was happiest of all when the prince thanked her for breaking the spell which had turned him into such a dreadful creature. They fell in love with each other immediately and the princess was exceedingly glad that it was the prince she was to

marry and not the Red Bull of Norroway.

All the guests left their seats and pressed round to see the beautiful princess who had freed the handsome prince, and just when everyone was smiling happily, there was a loud clap of thunder – and the prince disappeared.

The lord and his guests looked in all the rooms of the castle for the missing prince, while servants went out with lanterns to search the stables and the grounds, but there was no sign of the young man anywhere.

"Stay with us tonight, and tomorrow my servants will escort ye back to your home," the lord begged.

The princess thanked him for his offer but said she could not rest because she knew the prince was in great danger, and having rescued him once and lost him, she must rescue him again and break the power of whoever it was that had enchanted him, and then she would marry him as she had promised.

Off she went into the cold and the dark, and many a weary mile she walked until she could go no farther, and then she lay down in a grassy clearing where harebells grew and there she slept.

At daylight she drank from a nearby burn, ate a handful of wild berries to stay her hunger and continued on her search. When it began to grow dark again she knew she could walk no farther, and seeing ahead of her a cottage and a light shining from the window, she stumbled to it and knocked at the door.

"May a poor traveller beg food and shelter for the night?" she asked the wrinkled old woman who peered out at her.

"Poor wee lassie," the old woman said, drawing her in and closing the door. "Sit ye down by the fire and warm yourself, and presently we shall share my supper, and for the night ye shall have a bed of fresh straw."

It was hard to tell who was the more content now – the princess to be cared for or the old woman to do the caring, and as the princess told her story, the old woman nodded her head, saying "Poor wee lassie!" and "Bonny wee lassie!' from time to time.

When she awoke the next morning the princess was greatly refreshed and eager to continue her search for the prince she had glimpsed so briefly but with whom she had fallen so deeply in love.

"Take these with you," the old woman said, giving her three nuts. "But do not break them until your heart is like to break and owre again like to break. Now follow the path that winds through yon wood and down the brae: cross the burn by the stepping stones and ahead ye will see a fair highway. May God speed ye and bring ye to a safe conclusion."

Off the princess went, sometimes hopeful and sometimes sad, for the world was wide and she did not know where to find her lost love: all she knew was that she must go on searching until she found him or perish in the attempt.

Through the wood she walked and down the brae; she crossed the burn by the stepping stones and presently she came to a fair highway. As she hesitated, wondering which direction to take, a company of lords and ladies rode past, laughing and talking, and bells jingled as the horses tossed their heads. From the scraps of conversation she overheard, the princess gathered they were all wedding guests, but where the wedding was to be held, and who were the bride and groom she had no idea.

I might as well go in the same direction, she thought, and along the highway she walked.

Presently another company of lords and ladies overtook her, laughing and talking, and bells jingled as the horses tossed their heads, and this time the princess heard one of the ladies say that it was the rich and powerful Duke of Norroway who was to be married, and that the feast to follow would be the most magnificent and lavish ever known.

It was not long after this that she came to a splendid castle, and here there was a hustle and bustle of cooks and pastry-makers, kitchen maids and scullions, butchers and gamekeepers and gardeners, and though everyone was hurrying about busily, no one seemed to know where to go or just what should be done.

While the princess was watching all this confusion and thinking that it was extremely unlikely that a feast would be ready that day, she heard the sound of galloping hoofs and of barking dogs, as a party of ladies and gentlemen who had been out hunting returned, and a loud voice shouted, "Make way for the Duke of Norroway."

Curious to see this rich and powerful duke who was to be married that day, she stepped to one side and watched as the riders approached. Pale she grew and paler still as she saw her lover ride past without a glance in her direction, all his attention on the beautiful lady who rode with him.

Alas, she thought, remembering the words of the old woman in the cottage, the time has come sooner than I thought when my heart is like to break and owre again like to break.

And so she broke the first nut, and out came a wee wifie carding.

Into the castle she walked and asked to see the beautiful lady, and when she was taken up to her room, she said no word but held out her hand with the wee wifie combing wool so industriously.

Immediately the beautiful lady clapped her hands with delight.

"That is something I surely must have," she said. "What money or jewels do ye want for her?"

"All the money and jewels in the kingdom would not be enough," the princess answered. "But willingly will I give her to ye – on one condition."

"Yes?" the lady asked eagerly, watching the wee

wifie working so busily.

"Put off your wedding for twenty-four hours, and let me sit alone in the prince's room tonight."

So determined was the lady to have the wee wifie that she agreed straightaway, and off she went with her toy, which she hid in her room before going to see the prince.

"Events have been too much for ye, my dearie," she said, and sweeter than any honey was her voice. "Let us put off our wedding until tomorrow. Tonight I shall give ye a sleeping draught so that in the morning ye will awaken refreshed and ready to ride to the hunt again."

When at last it was midnight and everyone in the castle was asleep, the princess made her way to the room of the duke and sat down beside him. First she sighed, and then she wept and then she began to sing:

Far hae I sought ye, near am I brought to ye,
Dear Duke o' Norroway, will ye no' turn and
                                        speak to me?

Again and again she sighed and wept and sang, but not once did the duke stir or waken, and at the first cockcrow she had to leave him, and he not knowing that there had been anyone in his room.

That day she roamed about the gardens in great unhappiness, knowing that her heart was like to break and owre again like to break, and at last she took the second of the nuts and broke it, and out came a wee wifie spinning.

Into the castle she went and asked to see the lady, and when she was taken to her room, she said no word but held out her hand with the wee wifie spinning wool so industriously.

"That is something I must have," the lady declared.

"What money or jewels do ye want for her?"

"All the money and jewels in the kingdom would not be enough," the princess answered. "But willingly will I give her to ye if ye will put off your wedding for another twenty-four hours, and let me sit alone in the prince's room tonight."

So determined was the lady to have the wee wifie that she agreed straightaway, and then went and told the prince how tired he looked and that she had decided to put off their wedding and she would give him a sleeping draught that night.

When at last it was midnight and everyone in the castle was asleep, the princess made her way to the room of the duke and sat down beside him. First she sighed, and then she wept and then she began to sing:

> Far hae I sought ye, near am I brought to ye,
> Dear Duke of Norroway, will ye no' turn and
> > speak to me?

Again and again she sighed and wept and sang but not once did the duke stir or awaken, and at the first cockcrow she had to leave him, and he not knowing that there had been anyone in his room.

All day she roamed about the gardens, even more distraught then ever, and knowing that her heart was like to break and owre again like to break, she cracked the last of her nuts, and out came a wee wifie reeling.

As soon as the lady saw the wee wifie winding her wool so industriously she declared she must have her and agreed to the same conditions as before.

In the meantime, however, the duke's servant mentioned to his master that several times during the previous two nights he had been awakened by the sighing, weeping and singing coming from his master's room.

"Sighing, weeping and singing?" the duke repeated. "I heard nothing. Nothing at all."

"Do not take the sleeping draught which your lady will give ye tonight, and ye will hear what I have heard," the servant advised.

The duke bore his servant's words in mind, and though he accepted the sleeping draught, he poured it out of the window the moment the lady had left him, and then lay down on his bed, closed his eyes, and waited.

At midnight the princess came into the room, sat down, sighed, wept and then began to sing:

> *Far hae I sought ye, near am I brought to ye,*
> *Dear Duke o'Norroway, will ye no' turn and*
> *speak to me?*

"Now I know the voice and the singer too," the duke cried, starting up.

"Once again ye have removed the spell that was cast over me and wiped out my memory. At last I am free for ever."

Who exactly the enchantress was no one knew, but when the lady whom the duke had been about to marry left the castle that night and was never heard of again, the courtiers put two and two together and all agreed that because of the loyalty of the princess, the duke had had a very lucky escape.

As all the preparations for a wedding had been made, and the adventures of the Red Bull of Norroway had come to an end, the duke married the princess who had loved him so long, searched for him so patiently and rescued him twice from the power of an enchantress.

Killmoulis

At a time when birds and animals still talked and all kinds of strange creatures dwelt in the land, there lived in the Lowlands of Scotland a wealthy miller, his wife and daughter, his young apprentice – and also Killmoulis.

Some folk said Killmoulis was a bogle and others a brownie, but whatever he was they agreed he was not of the race of Man but a strange creature who could work hard if he felt like it: he was quick to take offence however, and at such times would sulk and do no work at all. He had a long memory, both for those who went out of their way to please him and for those who showed harm to anyone he liked.

Each night he slept in front of the killogee – the space in front of the fire in the kiln, where it was always warm, for if there was anything Killmoulis disliked, it was being cold.

When it pleased him, he would lend a hand with any job about the mill and on occasion, when a mill-stone was worn, he would do without his sleep to work all night, so that in the morning the stone was beautifully set and ready for work again.

Because he belonged to the Otherworld, not only could he see into the future and foretell marriages, but by wailing piteously he would also warn the miller and his family of approaching danger.

The miller was an honest enough fellow – for a miller. Whatever amount of oats or wheat or barley was brought to him, he would grind to flour and return most of it to the farmer, keeping only what he considered a reasonable quantity for himself.

The grinding of the millstones was music in his ear: when they were at work and the runner stone turning at a steady pace, they cried 'For-r pr-rofit . . . for-r pr-rofit,' and the miller rubbed his hands together with glee, but he frowned when the mill slowed down and the song changed to 'No pr-rofit . . . no pr-rofit.'

When he was not working at the mill and making money – some of which he hid in an old sock under the bed and the rest in a locked chest in the attic – then he and his wife would congratulate themselves on the beauty and kindness of their daughter who, they were convinced, would one day marry a prince.

The apprentice often glanced at the miller's daughter and sighed, while Killmoulis cared for her more than for anyone else, because she always fed him and found time to sit beside him and listen to his tales of goblins and redcaps and of witches who flew through the night on broomsticks or disguised themselves as simple country people – stories the old millwheel and the millstones used to whisper to him when ordinary people were fast asleep.

It was late one winter's night when there came a knock on the door of the cottage beside the mill, and when the apprentice opened the door there stood an old beggar woman, dressed all in black save for the red heels of her buckled shoes.

"A slice of bread to eat and a warm place to sleep for the night," she begged.

In the killogee in front of the kiln fire, Killmoulis wailed piteously.

But the miller was busy counting his money, his daughter was in bed and asleep and his wife – a kind woman – thought Killmoulis was sulking about some imagined slight. As for the apprentice, he did not know what to think, but for some reason he suddenly felt afraid.

The miller's wife cut several thick slices of bread of her own baking, spread them with butter and bramble jam of her daughter's making, and told the old woman she was welcome to sleep in the barn where there was plenty of straw to make her a bed.

Again Killmoulis wailed, but no one paid any attention to him. The miller was still counting his money, his daughter was asleep, and the old woman was muttering something beneath her breath, so that for some time all the miller's wife and the apprentice could hear was the song of the mill-race outside their door.

Early the next morning the miller's wife went down to feed her ducks in the bonny mill stream and again Killmoulis wailed.

Startled, the apprentice leaped from his bed and ran to the window, just in time to see the old woman push his mistress into the deep water, and by the time he had called out to his master and both had run to save her, it was too late. The miller's wife was drowned and the old woman had disappeared.

To save his daughter pain, the miller told his apprentice to say that her mother had slipped and fallen into the millstream, and this is what she believed.

For a long time the miller seemed to lose all interest in the mill, and he would sit and gaze into the mill-pond all day and sigh and shake his head. His daughter took over the housekeeping and the apprentice, with the help of Killmoulis, saw to the grinding of the flour and kept the machinery in good order.

At length the miller's daughter persuaded her father

to go to the nearby fair to meet old friends and win new orders. Reluctantly he set off, but no sooner had he arrived at the market place than he fell into conversation with a handsome widow whose own husband had been a miller and had died recently, leaving her – so she said – well provided for but lonely.

She was dressed all in black, as befitted a widow – save for the red heels of her buckled shoes.

Within three months the miller had married again, but when he brought his second wife back to the mill, Killmoulis wailed more piteously than ever before.

Nothing that the miller's daughter could say would make him stop and she, poor child, soon gave up trying to comfort him as she was heart-broken to find her mother's place filled so quickly.

The new stepmother, recognizing at once how great were Killmoulis' powers, decided she must act first.

"We cannot have Killmoulis making that noise day and night. You must get rid of him at once," she said to her husband, and though he demurred at first, in the end she got her way and, reluctantly, the miller gave Killmoulis a bag of meal and told him to find another mill as there was neither room nor work for him there.

The daughter, hearing what had happened, ran after him to bid him goodbye and offer him a bannock of her own baking and a jar of bramble jelly of her own making, and though he accepted her presents, all he said was "Killmoulis warned you," and away he went, stiff with anger and hurt pride.

By and by the apprentice came up, and finding the lassie weeping, dried her tears and told her not to be afraid, because he would always look after her. He did not like the new mistress either but he had not recognized her yet for what she was.

"So far, so good," the second wife said, watching

Killmoulis leave the mill. She bided her time until the day her husband went off to market and then she asked the lassie in a honey-sweet voice to walk with her by the bonny millstream, and the lassie, afraid though she knew not why, put down her sewing and went out with her stepmother.

When they reached the millrace the stepmother pointed to some blood-red poppies growing in a field on the opposite bank, and as the girl turned to look the stepmother pushed her into the deep water and, well satisfied, returned to the cottage, unaware that Killmoulis was hiding in the rushes and keeping the lassie's head above the water, or that the apprentice had run from the mill to help the two of them to safety.

"Now I recognize her," the apprentice said. "She is a witch and it was she who drowned your mother."

"If you had listened to me, none of this would have happened," Killmoulis pointed out.

And the lassie wept, because she knew that if she told her father about the stepmother's wickedness, he would not believe her, and she feared that the next time her stepmother tried to get rid of her, she would make sure the deed was accomplished properly, and then her father would forget all about her, just as he had forgotten about her mother.

"We must find a new home," the apprentice said, knowing that if they stayed in the end they would be powerless against a witch.

"What kind of a home?" the lassie asked.

"A mill of course," Killmoulis answered, and the apprentice nodded his head in agreement.

Together the three of them walked on and on and on, living on Killmoulis' meal boiled in water, picking herbs and berries and on occasion discovering wild honey and at night the apprentice found a shed or a

28

sheltered hollow where they slept, until at last they came to an old mill which had not been working for many a long year.

"This will do us," Killmoulis said.

"I shall light a fire for us," the apprentice said.

"And I shall make some porridge with the last of the meal," the lassie said.

After the meal Killmoulis gave the apprentice and the lassie an infusion of cowslips to drink, so that they slept deeply in front of the fire, but he drank nothing himself for there was much work to be done.

Although the mill had long been derelict he knew that the brownie who had once lived there might still be near and might resent intruders and try to make life impossible for them.

Out into the night he went and consulted a hunting owl, who agreed to find the brownie there and then, and when he appeared Killmoulis knew him to be one of the Wise Old Ones. It was soon obvious that the Old One had long felt lonely and neglected and was very pleased to think of new owners in the mill: he was quite willing to share the killogee with a stripling like Killmoulis, and together they smiled knowingly, aware that now the mill would have twice as much good luck as any other mill in the Lowlands.

"Of course we shall need help to get it into working order," Killmoulis pointed out.

"Yes," the Old One agreed. "And it must be finished before morning light. What about the miller and his young wife?"

"The miller is an apprentice for another year, and the lassie is the daughter of my former master and is wed to no one. But both have drunk deep of my infusion of cowslips and neither will waken until morning."

Hearing this, the Old One called out to the Little People of the Night – with whom he happened to be on good terms at that time – and told them exactly what was wanted.

Immediately the Little People laughed and clapped their hands and set to work with a will. They replaced roof tiles and window panes, mended doors and sills, pulled up rotting floor boards and put down new ones, checked the steps on the wooden ladders, renewed broken teeth in the cogwheels, cleaned the hopper, replaced broken floats on the great wooden millwheel and dressed the pair of wheat stones and the pair of barley stones. Through the dark night they sped like lightning, reaching out an empty hand into the air to close it a moment later on whatever was wanted – be it hammer or nails, wood or slates, saw or shovel or spade or wheelbarrow.

In the cottage was the sound of sawing and hammering, cutting and sewing, so that before long each bedroom was furnished and curtained, and downstairs in the kitchen were a table and chairs, a dresser and all kinds of wooden and pewter plates and dishes.

The box beside the fire was filled with logs and the one in the oven with salt. There was food in the larder and someone – either with, but more probably without, permission – had put seven laying hens in a shed and tethered a pair of goats to two trees in the orchard where the grass was long and green.

'Will she be safe now?'' the Little People of the Night asked, looking down at the sleeping lassie, for they had sensed Killmoulis' fears and now they shared them.

"I shall be here, and I can care for her," Killmoulis answered.

"Not all of the time," they pointed out.

"The apprentice – who will be a miller in one year's time – will be here and he can care for her."

"Not all of the time."

"I can make my home here and care for her," the black cat said, but the others shook their heads, knowing what power witches had over cats.

"We can make our home here and care for her," the mice said, but the others shook their heads, knowing that the mice would be too busy hunting for food and avoiding the cat.

"We can watch from our home under the eaves and care for her," the swallows said, but everyone knew they would leave the mill in the late summer and fly away to lands where there was no snow and the sun shone all day.

'I . . . am . . . always . . . here, the millwheel said in a deep voice. "I and the millrace, and together we shall watch over her and see she comes to no harm."

And that, everyone agreed, was the best suggestion of all, although privately Killmoulis made up his mind that he would see to things himself whenever possible.

When the lassie awoke the next morning, it was to the familiar sound of the wooden millwheel creaking as it turned, the roar of the water that drove it, the squeaking and protesting of old and new boards making acquaintance in the mill, the song of the wheels on the shaft which turned the millstones and the sweet smell of newly ground meal, still warm from the grinding.

Of course she asked the apprentice who had done all the work, but he was as astounded as she and hurried off to ask Killmoulis.

"Killmoulis is already at work with the Old One who used to live here," he said. "We must ask no questions but whatever happens you must not buy from anyone at the door or venture out alone even for a few steps, and on no account must you let your stepmother cross the threshold of the mill cottage."

"I will do whatever you and Killmoulis advise," the lassie agreed. "But I am most curious to know where the barley came from that is now being ground."

"That I cannot tell you, but this I do know – the next order I must win for myself."

Day after day he walked from farm to farm, telling whoever answered the door that the old mill was working again and asking if they had any corn to grind; but the farmers, afraid that he was too young and lacking in experience, shook their heads or offered such a small amount of wheat or barley that it was scarcely worth the apprentice's time taking it back to the mill.

However he accepted each order, no matter how small, with a cheerful smile and returned the full value of the ground meal the next day, keeping nothing back for himself, so that his customers were well pleased and word spread during the following market days that here at last was an honest miller.

Slowly the work increased and the runner stone, which at first had ground so little, singing 'No pr-rofit . . . no pr-rofit,' and often singing nothing at all, began to change its tune to 'Well ear-rned pr-rofit . . . well ear-rned pr-rofit.' Now the apprentice made enough money to buy extra food and tools and gear for the mill and lastly a pony and cart, and Killmoulis worked harder than ever before – which was just as well as the Old One had got out of the way of working and spent his time dozing in the sunshine or sleeping on the right-hand side of the killogee.

Meanwhile things had not been going well for the

miller. He missed his daughter and his apprentice and Killmoulis too, for they had all worked so hard for him, and his second wife was for ever wanting to be taken to markets and fairs where she spent money on this and that and the other.

He hired a new apprentice who was lazy and cheated him, and he kept on demanding more money from the farmers and helping himself to more of their meal, so that he found himself losing customers very quickly. It wasn't long before he had to dip into the first of his savings, which he kept in a sock under the mattress, and of course, it wasn't long before his second wife found the sock and began to help herself too.

Very soon the two fell a-quarrelling.

"It was an ill day when I met you," the miller declared. "I should have listened to what my apprentice said about you, and I should never have agreed to send Killmoulis away. If it had not been for that my daughter would never have fallen in the millrace and been drowned."

"Forget about your daughter," the second wife said. "Hire another man and get more work for the mill. Half the time it stands silent when it should be making money for the two of us."

"I shall never get more work. My old customers say I charge too much and now it appears they go to a mill farther down the river where the young owner is most industrious and charges a very fair rate, and his young sister offers ale and cheese of her own making while the farmers wait."

This is ill news, the stepmother thought.

"Does good luck go with the mill?" she asked.

"Twice as much as with any other," the miller answered.

And that is even worse news, she thought.

"I am going on a visit to see some relations I have not seen for a long time," she told her husband the next morning. "You may expect me back within seven days."

As soon as the miller had gone to market, she set to work and baked some delicious honey cakes, but in the centre of each she placed one drop of deadly poison, and then dressing herself in sober country clothes and wearing a bonnet which concealed most of her face, she set off with the basket of honey cakes over her arm and the buckled shoes with red heels peeping from underneath her skirts.

She walked on and she walked on and she walked on, but as it was past midwinter and there were neither berries nor fruits nor herbs for her to eat, and as she dared not taste even a mouthful of her own wares, she grew exceedingly hungry. She had no talent either for finding sheltered places in which to sleep, so that by the time she arrived at the mill, which she could see had been carefully and lovingly repaired, she was in truth in a sorry state.

To make quite sure she had found the right place however, she hid behind a briar bush by the millwheel and waited.

"That's one," she said, as Killmoulis came out of the cottage and went into the mill.

"And that's the other," she added, as the apprentice went off in the horse and trap. All I have to do, she thought, is get rid of the girl and then the miller, and the mill and all the gold that is hidden in the chest in the attic will be mine.

But the black cat, who had been asleep on the windowsill, wakened suddenly. His whiskers twitched once and with a loud miaow he launched himself at the stepmother, tearing the shoulder and sleeve of her

35

gown to ribbons before making for the mill.

Loudly the stepmother screeched with pain and fright.

At the sound of the cat's miaow and the stepmother's screech, one of the mice peered out of its hole: his whiskers twitched twice and then he ran up the stepmother's dress, circled her neck and ran down her arm while she screamed again and again and again.

Alarmed by the noise, the lassie opened her door and looked out. Immediately her stepmother stopped screaming. And waited. And put thoughts into the lassie's head.

Forgetting the apprentice's warning, the lassie stepped out and went across to the countrywoman standing by the millwheel.

"Buy my honey cakes," the stepmother quavered in an old, old voice.

But now the lassie remembered how she had been warned never to buy from anyone at the door.

"No, thank you," she said, taking a step back.

"Then accept one as a present and taste how good it is," the stepmother wheedled, her eyes fixed on the lassie and glittering under her bonnet. Reluctantly the lassie stretched out her hand to take the proffered cake, but at that moment the millwheel groaned louder than it had ever groaned before. Startled, the stepmother turned and slipped, whereupon the millwheel struck her with first one and then another of its wooden floats and sent her flying into the millstream, where the river seized her and carried her off – and Killmoulis, hurrying out of the mill, was just in time to see a pair of red-heeled shoes disappearing beneath the fast-flowing water, while brown honey buns bobbed along until at last they too sank to the river bed.

The miller waited seven days and then another seven and when his second wife did not return, he heaved a sigh of relief for, to tell the truth, he was heartily tired of her. Selling his mill to the first buyer, he went off with his chest of gold to live in a far-away country, but what happened to him after that no one knows.

The apprentice, the lassie and Killmoulis, helped by the luck of the Old One, of course, did so well that not long after the apprentice had become a miller, they knew that they were well on the way to being rich.

It was early one Saturday evening that Killmoulis closed one eye, stood on one leg and said, "There will be a wedding here soon."

Neither the lassie nor the young miller – who had once been the apprentice – said anything, but the very next day a prince happened to ride past with his courtiers, and seeing the lassie, fell in love with her on the spot and offered to marry her there and then.

"What did I tell you?" Killmoulis whispered to the young miller – who had once been the apprentice.

The young miller did not look at all pleased but they both watched as the lassie curtseyed and thanked the prince for the honour he had done her. "But truth to tell," she added, "I am to be wed on Saturday."

"Who are you to wed?" the young miller asked angrily, as the prince and his courtiers rode away.

"You of course," the lassie answered.

And wed they were on Saturday, and they and their children lived happily ever after at the mill, cared for by Killmoulis, the Old One, the birds and the animals and all the Little People of the Night.

The Milkmaid of Whittingham

Long ago when there were fairies and witches and all kinds of strange creatures who might bring good luck if they were in a good temper but could cause all manner of trouble if they were not, there lived at Whittingham, a village in the far north of England, a milkmaid with long, nut-brown hair.

Her hands were as smooth as butter, as white as milk, and as cool as spring water, and because she was both pretty and good-natured, there were many young men who sighed for her, calling her the bonniest milkmaid in all Northumberland, begging her to marry them and swearing that if she did not, they would surely die.

The maid, however, always shook her head, saying that she could not marry one and cause the death of all the others. So tactfully did she refuse them and so attractive was she when she smiled afterwards, that everyone loved her the more, and no one dreamed she had already fallen in love with a young man she had seen only for a few seconds the previous year at Whittingham Fair.

Who he was and where he came from she did not know, but she was content to wait until the following August, convinced that he would come to the Fair again, see her and fall in love with her, as all the other young men had done.

Meanwhile she cared for her master's cows, calling

each by its own name, so that they loved her as much as did the young men and yielded more milk than they did for any other milkmaid.

Her mistress declared that her cream was twice as thick and delicious as that of her neighbours, her butter of a finer quality and flavour than that of anyone else, while the buttermilk always smelled sweetly of thyme and meadowgrass: as for her cheeses, both soft and hard, they won praise from all who tasted them.

Often she was asked how it was that her milk and cream, her butter, buttermilk and cheeses were of such a high quality, and each time she curtseyed, smiled, but said nothing.

But she knew.

Of course she knew.

Her mother had told her, and her grandmother had told her mother.

Every night, before she went to bed, she left a bowl of rich, creamy milk on the dairy step: every morning the bowl was empty, and she was sure the fairy people had helped themselves. Because they were pleased with her she was sure they would always help her in her work and would do her no harm.

A fortnight before the Fair, the wandering piper and his lad arrived at the farm, as they did each year. As soon as the day's work was done, everyone gathered in the big, stone-flagged kitchen, listening eagerly as the piper gave them news of all that had happened in Northumberland and the Border Country throughout the past months, and then, to the accompaniment of pipe music, the lad sang the old ballads of Border battles and the sad songs of maidens deserted by false lovers.

Finally the piper played a new air, and the boy hummed an accompaniment, but when his listeners asked its name and what words there were to it, the piper shook his head.

"It is a tune that came to me today as we were on our way to Whittingham Fair, so that is its name. When I come next year, doubtless I shall have found words to fit to it."

On the day before the Fair everyone worked twice as hard as usual so that there would be little to do on the morrow, and so excited and tired was the milkmaid that she quite forgot to leave the bowl of rich, creamy milk on the dairy step.

The next day the master, the mistress, the dairymaid and all who could be spared from the farm work went down to Whittingham Fair and mingled with old friends who had come from Alnwick and Rothbury, Thropton and Alwinton, Eslington and Callaly and many other villages, hamlets and farms.

There masters hired new men and men found new masters, and everyone crowded round the stalls to buy what they needed – apples, gooseberries and nuts, butter, eggs and cheese, hats and caps and knives and spoons: the lads bought stockings and buckles for themselves and ribbons and lace for their sweethearts, and the maids bought needles and thread for themselves and sweetmeats and gingerbread for the lads they favoured.

All day the milkmaid searched for the young man she had fallen in love with the previous year, but it was not until the fiddlers began to tune up for the first dance that she saw him making his way towards her through the crowd.

"Will you partner me in this dance?" he asked, and she smiled and gave him her hand.

Three times they danced together, and though they spoke but little, the maid was sure the young man loved her as much as she did him. Because she did not want him to think she lacked partners, she turned away at the fourth dance and gave her hand to a forester who had loved her long.

The dancers had all taken their places and the fiddlers had lifted their bows for the opening chords when suddenly everyone fell silent and the crowd parted to let through a beautiful lady. Corn gold was her hair and grass green the silken robe which whispered with each light step she took. Walking straight up to the young man, she stared into his eyes; without a word he led her to the dance, and only when they had taken their place did the fiddlers begin to play.

And how they played!

It was as though they were bewitched – fiddlers and dancers and onlookers too. Time lost all meaning: all cares and troubles were forgotten. The old felt young again, and the young felt like kings and queens – until suddenly there was a clap of thunder, and everyone stood still and stared around in bewilderment, wondering what had possessed them. Only the milkmaid, searching anxiously through the silent dancers, realized the lady in green and the young man were no longer there.

At the same moment she recalled she had not left out the bowl of creamy milk the previous night; she knew now that the fairy people were her enemies and that it was the Fairy Queen herself who had stolen her love away.

Month after month she went about her work, and though the cream was good, the butter reasonable, the buttermilk satisfactory and the cheeses fair enough, her mistress and master were concerned that she seemed troubled, and the lads and lasses whispered that something ailed her and no longer was she the

41

bonniest milkmaid in all Northumberland.

Every night she left out the bowl of creamy milk, but each morning it was untouched and the maid knew the fairy people had not forgiven her.

Exactly a year after their last visit, the piper and his boy arrived at the farm again, bringing with them all the local news. Again the lad sang the old ballads of Border battles and the sad songs of maids deserted by false lovers, and then the piper played the tune which was both sad and merry. When his listeners asked if he had found words to it, he nodded his head.

"There are words indeed, but not of my making, and there is a tale to those words well worth the telling.

"It was late last night and the lad and I were weary for we had travelled far that day, and at length we decided to rest awhile on Fawdon Hill."

His audience held their breaths and exchanged furtive glances, for they knew about Fawdon Hill and there was not a man or woman amongst them who would have gone near it once the sun had set.

"We lay in a little hollow, but before sleep claimed us, a door in the hill opened: the air was filled with music such as I had never heard before and a host of fairy people crowded out to dance by the white light of the moon.

"Two of the dancers I had seen before. The lady wore a gown of grass green silk and on her head was a golden crown, and the young man who partnered her gazed at her with strange, wild eyes.

"And then the lad sneezed.

"Everyone stopped dancing. The lady touched the young man on the shoulder and he turned towards us and sang, and though the air was mine and a year old, the words were of his own making."

42

The piper lifted the pipe to his lips again and the lad sang:

Are you going to Whittingham Fair?
Parsley, sage, rosemary and thyme.
Remember me to one who lives there
For once she was a true love of mine.

Tell her to make me a cambric shirt,
Parsley, sage, rosemary and thyme,
Without any seam or needlework,
For once she was a true love of mine.

As the music and the song died away, the milkmaid wiped away a single tear from each eye and lifted up her head proudly.

"That is only part of your song, piper," she said. "Come to the Fair next week and I shall sing you other verses more to my liking."

Now she knew that the only person who could help her was the Wise Woman of Cheviot, but what her price would be she dared not guess.

The next evening, with the permission of her mistress, she filled a basket with eggs, butter, cheese and freshly baked bread, and climbed up the hillside until she came to a thatched cottage.

"The door is on the latch. Walk in," a voice cried before the maid had even lifted her hand to knock.

The maid did as she was bid, and by the light of the fire she saw the Wise Woman sitting on a wooden stool. Curtseying, she placed the basket on the floor and waited while the Wise Woman looked first at its contents and then at her.

"And what makes you think I can help you win back your true love when it was your forgetfulness and vanity which delivered him into the power of the Fairy

Queen?" she demanded.

"If you cannot help me, no one can," the maid answered, not at all surprised to find the Wise Woman knew why she had come.

"What was the message he sent you by the piper and his lad?" the Wise Woman asked.

Softly, sadly, the maid sang her true love's song.

" 'A cambric shirt, without any seam or needlework'," the Wise Woman said. "Yes, I can make that, but how high a price are you prepared to pay?"

"Whatever you ask," the maid replied.

"Give me your nut-brown hair which you brush so carefully each night and which everyone admires."

The maid hesitated, sighed, and bent her head so that the Wise Woman could cut off her hair of which she was so proud.

The Wise Woman laughed.

"Keep your locks, milkmaid. It is enough for me to know you are willing to part with them without protest to win back your love."

"Now listen carefully, for my magic will work only if you do exactly as I tell you. On the day before the Fair, break off a twig from the rowan tree which grows by the stream, and gather a nosegay of certain herbs. At nightfall go to Fawdon Hill" – pausing, she peered at the maid. "Are you afraid to go to the fairy people's dancing place, alone, and at night?"

"Yes," the maid answered, "but I will go in spite of that."

"Good. Hide behind the blackberry bush on the right of the track and wait until the dance has begun. Your love will stand apart from the others, waiting to partner the Fairy Queen. When she comes out of the hill she will have to pass the blackberry bush to reach him. At the moment she is nearest to you, stand up,

grasp your rowan twig firmly and sing the words which come to your tongue. Afterwards, use your nosegay of herbs wisely.

"Go straight back to the farm alone and put out the bowl of rich, creamy milk on the dairy step. Place your kerchief beside it. When you awake in the morning you will find the bowl empty and the cambric shirt wrapped in your kerchief. Do not unwrap it, but take it with you to the Fair and give it to your love when he comes to you."

Again the maid curtseyed, and as she ran back to the farm, she went over in her mind all the Wise Woman had told her to do.

The day before the Fair, she broke off a twig from the rowan tree which grew by the stream, gathered a nosegay of certain herbs, and at nightfall set off for Fawdon Hill. She had just hidden behind the blackberry bush on the right of the track, when a door in the hillside opened and the fairy people danced out to the most enchanting music. Silently the maid watched as her true love, now dressed in fine silk and velvet, stood apart from the others.

At last the Fairy Queen appeared in her gown of grass green silk and as she passed the blackberry bush, the maid stood up and grasped her rowan twig firmly, knowing it would protect her against the magic of the fairies.

Immediately the music ceased and the dancing stopped, and in the silence which followed the maid tossed back her head proudly and sang the words which came to her tongue:

> When he has done and finished his work,
> Parsley, sage, rosemary and thyme,
> O, tell him to come and he'll have his shirt,
> For once he was a true love of mine.

46

Tell him to find me an acre of land,
Parsley, sage, rosemary and thyme,
And sow it all over with one peppercorn,
For once he was a true love of mine.

Realizing that the maid was protected by a magic greater than her own, the Fairy Queen stamped her foot and then struck the young man on his cheek so that he fell to the ground as though dead. There was a loud clap of thunder and for a moment the whole place was covered in darkness: when the moon appeared again, the Fairy Queen and all her people had disappeared, and the maid was alone on the dancing ground with her true love at her feet.

Kneeling down, she took from her nosegay some fretted parsley and placed it on the young man's eyes.

"This will help you to distinguish between this world and that of the fairy people, when you awaken," she said.

Next she took some grey-green sage and placed it on his forehead.

"This will help your memory, so that you will remember all that happened in this world, and forget what is best forgotten in the world of the fairy people."

Now she chose some sweet-smelling rosemary, and put it in his right hand.

"This will waken you from your magic sleep, so that you will be as you were when we two danced together at Whittingham Fair."

And the last of her nosegay, the sweet-scented thyme, she placed above his heart.

"This will restore the breath of life that the Fairy Queen would fain have taken away."

Even as he stirred and sighed and remembered, the maid was up and running back to the farm, to fall asleep the moment her head touched the pillow.

The next morning she found on the dairy step the empty bowl and her kerchief, and remembering what the Wise Woman had said, she did not unwrap the kerchief although she greatly longed to see the cambric shirt. Carrying it carefully, she went down to the Fair with the master, the mistress and all who could be spared from the farm, and mingled with old friends who had come from Alnwick and Rothbury, Thropton and Alwinton, Eslington and Callaly, and everyone crowded round the stalls that sold apples, gooseberries and nuts, butter, eggs and cheese, hats and caps and knives and spoons.

As for the maid, she did not search for her true love, because she knew that this year he would come to her.

It was just as the fiddlers struck up the first dancing tune that he walked up to her. Everyone stared, because while they were all in their best clothes, he had come in the old breeches and shirt he wore when working on the land, and his face and hands were streaked with soil.

"Today I have done and finished my work," he said, "and now I have come for my cambric shirt."

The maid held out her kerchief.

"It is in there." Taking it, the young man sighed.

"How can I find an acre of land and sow it all over with one peppercorn?" he asked. "Must I lose you even though I do not deserve you?"

The farmer's wife turned to her husband.

"I do not want to lose the best milkmaid there is in all Northumberland, and you said only this morning that you could do with more help on the land." And she lowered her voice and whispered in his ear.

Smiling, the farmer nodded his head.

"Young man," he said, "I have a mind to hire

another farm worker. There is a fine cottage now vacant, and an acre of land I would rent for – one peppercorn!

"If you are a good worker you will have a fair wage and corn enough to sow your land.

"There is just one other little matter. It was a married couple I had in mind for my cottage."

Whereupon the young man, in front of all the crowd at Whittingham Fair, asked the maid to marry him, and of course, the maid accepted him.

At that everyone cheered and clapped, and as the fiddlers struck up the first dance, the young man placed the kerchief, with the shirt in it, on the grass, and led the maid on to the green.

All evening they danced together, she in her best dress and he in his working clothes. Once the maid thought she glimpsed the Wise Woman amongst the crowd, but when she looked again the old woman had gone.

At the end of the last dance they went, hand in hand, for the kerchief and the cambric shirt, but both had disappeared. The maid found her kerchief on the dairy step the next morning, but no one ever saw the cambric shirt again.

In fact, now I come to think of it, no one had ever seen it at all!

However, the dairymaid married her true love and they both lived happily ever after, and that is all that matters, isn't it?

The Outlandish Knight

Long ago, when there was magic in the land, there lived a king with one fair daughter whom he loved almost as much as he did his hawk, his hound and the three and thirty horses in his stables.

He would have preferred a son, but as his wife died soon after the birth of his daughter he decided that there was no reason why the child should not grow up to be a companion for him.

From an early age, therefore, she was taught to ride and hunt and to shoot with a bow and arrow, and had it not been for the protests of the older Court ladies, she would have been allowed to wrestle and to use a sword.

By the time she was of an age to marry, many young men, hearing how fair she was and how generous would be her dowry – for the king, her father, was extremely rich – journeyed from afar and presented themselves at Court, desirous of wooing and winning her. But each in turn discovered that no matter how hard he could ride, how true and keen the flight of his arrow, the princess could outride and outshoot everyone, and whether the hunt might be for a stag, wild boar, fox, badger or hare, she would leave her suitor behind after the first few minutes and be at the kill by her father's side at the end of the day.

Thus suitors came – and suitors departed, for no young man liked to find himself beaten in all the knightly sports by a princess, no matter how fair she might be. The king was unconcerned as he was in no mind to lose the company of such a brave and fearless daughter, but the princess began to worry lest she should find no man worthy of her.

One winter's day, when for long the nights had been dreary and dark and the days so cold and wet that it had been impossible to ride abroad, the princess retired to her room to talk to the parrot which she kept in a hand-carved cage of wood, hung high in her window. This parrot she loved dearly, partly because he was old and wise, but chiefly because he listened long and spoke but little.

"I am weary of these days when my maids sew fine seams and sing sweet songs and are content to stay indoors. I long for the Spring when I can ride and hunt and do those deeds at which I excel, but yet I fear that no suitor will present himself who will be my equal."

"Perhaps the time has come to think less of sport and more of yourself," the parrot answered at length. "Send for the tailor, the seamstress, the shoemaker and the fashioner of stockings. Tell them you want a splendid velvet gown edged with fur, a petticoat of holland linen, a headdress of finest lawn, stockings of silk and slippers of the softest leather."

The princess, who had hitherto concerned herself but little with fine clothes, preferring what was most serviceable for a life out-of-doors to what most became her, now clapped her hands with pleasure and went out there and then to give her orders. What with choosing materials and discussing styles, trying on, fitting, changing her mind about this and wondering whether or not to have that, the last of the cold wet days of winter passed, and on the very first day that the skies cleared that year and the sun shone on the Spring flowers, the princess appeared in her petticoat of holland linen, her splendid velvet gown edged with fur, her headdress of finest lawn, her silk stockings and slippers of softest leather.

"She is without doubt the loveliest princess in all the land," the courtiers, knights, ladies-in-waiting and pages whispered – but loud enough for the princess to hear, of course.

As she smiled she noticed a stranger at the far end of the hall.

"Who is that man?" she asked.

"That is the Outlandish Knight," her maid answered.

His armour shone in the sunlight and he carried his helmet under one arm so that all might see how fair was his hair, how blue his eyes, how proud his look.

Advancing, he bowed to the king, kissed the hand of the princess and then leading her to one side, he began to talk to her, all the time looking down into her eyes. All day they talked and all evening, but what was the subject of their conversation no one could say, as their voices were low and they remained apart from the others.

"I am content, my pretty parrot," the princess said, when she retired to her room that evening and she did not care when the parrot made no reply.

Down in the courtyard a predatory cat mewed softly, and the parrot listened but still said nothing.

On the next day the princess was up with the sun and she invited the Outlandish Knight to join her in a day's hunting for a noble stag.

"Nothing would please me more," he said, "but I have journeyed long and my horse is tired and lame."

"Come with me and take your pick from my father's stables," she offered, whereupon he chose a fine dapple grey and she mounted her milk white steed.

The hounds gave tongue, the horn was blown and

the hunt was off, the king, the princess and the Outlandish Knight in the lead.

Greatly to the surprise of the princess, the Outlandish Knight kept up with her and her father the whole day long, and was there with them when they found and killed in the evening.

"I am more than content, my pretty parrot," the princess said, when she retired to her room that evening, and she did not care when the parrot made no reply.

Down in the courtyard the cat mewed loudly and the parrot fluttered his wings and decided that now the time had come to speak.

"I know whom to fear and I hope that you do too, my mistress," he said.

"I do not understand you, my pretty parrot," the princess answered carelessly. "But you have no cause to fear: you are quite safe in your hand-carved cage of wood, so high in my window."

On the following day the princess was again up with the sun, and this time she went with the Outlandish Knight to the butts in the castle grounds. Three times she fitted her yard long arrows, feathered from the gay peacock, to her bow of yew, which was exactly her height, and soon the three arrows sat together in the centre of the target: whereupon the Outlandish Knight let fly his arrows and each clove in two one of the princess's wands of elm, so that she knew then that in all ways he was her equal.

That evening they talked again, the Outlandish Knight and the princess.

"Never have I known a princess as fearless and as beautiful as you," he said. "But I, alas! am poor, and have little to offer a wife save a castle and wide lands in the Outlandish Country, which lies between England

54

and Scotland, and which some call the Debateable Lands, because throughout the years my countrymen and yours have fought for their ownership."

"A castle and wide lands is all that I would ask," the princess answered. "I have my mother's jewels and my father will give me gold enough for two."

The Outlandish Knight shook his head sadly.

"I fear the king will want a wealthier husband than I for his only daughter."

"My father will accept the man that I want – in time," the princess answered proudly.

"Then come away with me tonight and we shall be married in my own country. Ride your milk white steed and lend me the dapple grey as my own horse is tired and lame and not fit for a knight such as I. Wear your finest clothes and bring your mother's jewels and your father's gold, and you shall rule in my castle and ride and hunt in my wide lands in the Outlandish Country."

"I am come to say farewell to you, my pretty parrot," the princess said when she returned to her room that evening, and instead of going to bed she dressed in her petticoat of holland linen, her splendid velvet gown edged with fur, her headdress of finest lawn and her silken stockings and slippers of softest leather.

Round her neck and on her arms she wore her mother's jewellery and in a bag she placed as much of her father's gold as she could carry, and so concerned was she with all this that she did not hear the cat mewing loudly in the courtyard, nor did she hear his sharp claws scratching as he tried to climb the wall beneath her window.

"Alas! Alas!" cried the parrot in its wooden cage, high up in the window, but the princess would not stay to listen and closing the door behind her, she crept quietly down to the stables, where the Outlandish Knight awaited her. There she mounted her milk white steed and he the dapple grey, and after he had fastened the bag of gold to his saddle they rode off together into the night.

On they rode in the starlight, and on and on, until at last, just as the moon appeared, they came to the mouth of a deep, wide river where the cold salt water of the sea flowed in to meet the fresh water from the high hills, and the banks on both sides were steep and rugged.

"Light off your beautiful milk white steed and give her over to me," the Outlandish Knight cried as he himself dismounted, and proud and handsome – and wicked – he now looked in the pale moonlight. "My castle – such as it is, and my lands – such as they are – lie on the far side of this broad river, but you shall never see them. Six pretty maidens have I drowned here, and you, methinks, will be the seventh." And he stood between the princess and the river, barring the way to the Outlandish Country, which some call the Debateable Lands.

As she dismounted, the jewels the princess wore sparkled like the stars in the sky, and long and loud laughed the Outlandish Knight.

"Take off your mother's jewels and give them all to me," he cried. "And take off too your velvet gown and headdress of lawn, for they are too rich to rot beneath the sea."

Slowly and without speaking, the princess took from her arms and her neck her mother's jewels and placed each piece on the grass beside her, and then she stood up straight in the moonlight and looked at the Outlandish Knight proudly: and when she spoke her voice was as cold as the cold salt water of the sea.

"You called yourself a knight when you came to my father's Court, and like a knight were you treated. If I must take off my velvet gown, then behave like that knight you claim to be and turn your back on me."

The Outlandish Knight dropped his eyes, and if ever he felt ashamed of himself, he felt ashamed then, and if ever he felt sorrow for a fair maid, he felt sorrow then, and turning his back on the princess, he stared across the wide mouth of the river and saw the salt water flooding in.

Whereupon the princess took three quick, light steps forward and, with all the strength of hands and arms which had learned to control a mettlesome horse and to bend a splendid bow of yew and let fly arrows one yard long – she pushed the Outlandish Knight so that he fell headlong over the bank and down into the deep, wide river.

Down he sank and down, and then he struggled to the surface and flung up one mailed arm:

> *"Catch hold of my hand, my pretty maiden*
> *And I will make you my bride,"*

he cried, and his voice was that of a desperate man.

> *"Catch hold of my hand, my pretty maiden*
> *And I will make you my bride,"*

he cried a second time,
But the princess shook her head and laughed.

> *"Lie there, lie there, you false-hearted man,*
> *Lie there instead of me;*
> *Six pretty maids have you drowned here,*
> *And the seventh has drownèd thee."*

Loud shrieked the Outlandish Knight as the weight of his shining armour bore him down and when the cold dark sea had closed over him, the princess laughed again. "The seventh has drownèd thee," she repeated, and replacing her mother's jewellery round her neck and arms, she mounted her milk white steed and with the dapple grey beside her she rode back the way she had come.

It wanted but an hour to daybreak when at last she stole into her room, but before she had begun to take off her velvet gown her parrot cried loudly from its wooden cage high in the window, "Where have you been and why were you away so long? All night have I been awake because I feared you were in deadly danger."

"Not so loud, my pretty parrot," the princess whispered. "It is true that I was in deadly danger but all is well now, and if you will promise not to prittle or prattle or to tell any one that I was gone from my room this night, you shall have a cage of glittering gold."

At that moment, in the next room the king, who had been awakened by the sound of voices, called out:

"What ails you, what ails you, my pretty parrot,
That you prattle so long before day?"

"I am sorry I wakened you," the parrot answered. "I called out loudly because I was afraid. For three nights there has been a cat in the courtyard below and I thought it had climbed into this room to kill – "he paused and looked at the princess."To kill me," he continued, "but it was only a cloud which crossed the moon and cast a shadow on the floor."

"A clever answer, my pretty parrot," the princess whispered. "A clever answer, indeed, and one that has saved me from explaining how foolish and mistaken I was these last three days. And for that:

Thy cage shall be made of the glittering gold,
And the door of the best ivory."

"And the cat?" the parrot asked softly.

"He will trouble you no more. He sleeps where he drowned six pretty maidens," the princess answered. "He was my equal in sport and in the chase, I admit, but it was I who thought the quicker and acted on the thought, so that I am here alive while he lies dead beneath the cold, salt sea."

The King and the Miller of Tweed

Once upon a time there lived a miller on the north bank of the River Tweed, which separates Scotland from England. He wasn't a very clever man, but he did a fair day's work himself and saw that Jock, his apprentice, did twice as much: he had one daughter, a shrewd lassie, who cooked and cleaned and kept a careful eye on the money her father made – and on Jock too, for the apprentice was a fine, good-looking lad, though inclined to be shy and not much given to talking.

Now one day, when the miller was sitting on the river bank having a wee rest, he heard the sound of spurs and bridles jingling and men shouting to one another, and getting to his feet he saw a party of soldiers approaching on horseback. Strangers they were, all of them, and wealthy judging by their arms and fine clothes, and it didn't take the miller long to realize that the man at the head was a duke or some kind of a nobleman, or even a king, though what a king would be doing up here in the North Country he just couldn't imagine. So he took off his cap and waited.

"Are ye the miller?" the leader asked.

"Aye," the miller answered.

"Weel, I'm the king."

"Aye, Your Highness," the miller said, not knowing what else to say as he'd never met a king before.

"Being a king and ruling a country takes a great deal o' siller – and gowd too," the king said.

"I dare say it does, Your Highness," the miller agreed, wondering if he could say that being a miller took a great deal of silver and gold too, but deciding hastily that such a remark might not be very wise. "I dare say it does," he repeated nervously.

"And that's why I need a' your siller and gowd, your meal, your land and your mill."

The miller trembled and grew pale: in those days a king was a king and could do whatever he liked and not all the millers in the land could say him nay.

"But I'm a just man," the king continued, and he looked at his soldiers and they all nodded their heads in agreement. "I always give people a fair chance. So I'll tell ye what I'll do. I'll ask ye three questions, and if ye can answer them, ye can keep a' your siller and gowd, your meal, your land and your mill."

"I'm not what ye'd call a quick-thinking man, Your Highness," the miller stammered. "Especially not when it comes to answering questions of any kind." He mightn't be quick-thinking but well did he know that the questions the king would ask would be the kind that no one could answer. He'd set his heart on the miller's silver and gold, meal and land and mill, and he meant to have them.

"Ye'll not be rushed," the king assured him, smiling genially, for the longer he listened to the millwheel turning and the millstones grinding, and the more he saw of the mill itself and the surrounding land, the better pleased he was. "I'll ask ye the questions now and I'll come back in a year and a day for your answers. That's fair enough, isn't it?" he asked, appealing to his soldiers.

"Aye, Your Highness," they all said.

"Aye, Your Highness," the miller agreed, knowing that somehow it wouldn't be fair at all.

"Good. So here we go.

"First, I want to know the weight of the moon. Second, I want to know how many stars there are in the sky. And third, I want ye to tell me exactly what I'm thinking when I talk to ye again in a year and a day."

"Best see if I've got it right," the miller said slowly. "First ye want to know the weight of the moon. Second ye want to know how many stars there are in the sky. And third ye want me to tell ye exactly what ye're thinking the next time we meet."

"Aye, " the king agreed. "And I'll be back with my men in a year and a day." And away he and his soldiers rode, laughing heartily.

If I've got a year and a day to think of the answers, the miller thought, there's no point in worrying about them now. And so he didn't. Worry, I mean. Not at first, anyway. But the weeks passed and the months, and when he found that he couldn't think of an answer to any of the questions, he really did begin to worry.

It didn't take his daughter long to discover that something was the matter with the miller, but she knew it was no good asking outright because, although he wasn't clever, he liked to think he was; and so she did what she always did in such situations – she prepared his favourite meals, persuaded the lad to work even harder (and that wasn't difficult because he had just realized he was head over heels in love with her) and encouraged her father to relax and fish for salmon in the river.

It wasn't long before the miller, having had the

leisure in which to appreciate how fortunate he was to have such a profitable mill, grew so anguished at the thought of losing it that he had to tell the whole story to his daughter.

"So that's all that's worrying ye?" she said, when she'd heard his tale. "Everyone knows how clever ye are. I'm sure ye'll think of the answers before the time is up. All ye need is a wee bit of advice."

"What kind of advice?" the miller demanded. "If it's lawyers ye have in mind, I'd have ye know they're worse than any king. Before they'd answered the first question they'd have a' my siller and gowd, my meal, land and mill, the lad and ye too *and* they'd have me shut up in the debtor's prison."

"It's not lawyers I have in my mind. It's Jock, your lad. And it'll not cost ye a penny as he works for ye already."

"Jock? What advice can he give me?"

"Give him time and he'll think of something. I'll have a word with him myself, after he's finished his work. He may not talk much but he thinks a great deal."

It was dark before Jock had finished his work and as the miller watched his daughter and the lad strolling by the river in the moonlight, he hoped that Jock was thinking a great deal for he did not appear to say a single word.

"Weel?" he asked, when at last his daughter returned to the kitchen and Jock went off, sighing heavily, to his room.

"He says the questions are very difficult and he must have time to think about them. We are to meet again to discuss them tomorrow night."

After the meeting the following night the miller's daughter told her father that Jock still had not found the answers, but he was feeling very hopeful that he soon would, and so she had arranged to meet him again. And again and again and again.

What they talked about or if Jock talked at all, the miller had no idea, but just when it was almost time for the king's return visit the lad spoke up.

"When we go to Berwick market tomorrow," he said, "there are one or two things I have to buy for your daughter, from a wee shop in the High Street. I've to use the egg money, so it'll not be costing ye anything."

Jock bought whatever it was he'd been told to buy, and each evening he walked along the bank of the river with the miller's daughter, talking now, aye, and laughing too, while the miller himself grew more and more unhappy and despondent.

When the whole year had passed he could contain himself no longer.

"Tomorrow the king comes with his men to take away my siller and gowd, my meal and land and mill, and then it'll be the poorhouse for the three of us."

"If I can answer the three questions," Jock said, "and save your siller and gowd, your meal and land and mill, will ye let me marry your daughter and take me for your son-in-law?"

"Ye answer the questions?" the miller cried. "Ye could no more do that than the millwheel down there could turn itself."

"The millwheel turns with the help of the mill-stream," the lassie said, "and the miller's lad will answer the questions with the help of the miller's daughter. Let him try, Father. Do ye bide in bed tomorrow and leave the answering to Jock."

Because there was nothing else he could do the miller took to his bed there and then, slept not at all, and when the morrow came pulled the sheets over his head so that he could neither see nor hear when the king and his men rode up.

Jock, however, was very busy. First he dressed himself in an old suit of the miller's which the lassie had given him, and then he unwrapped the purchases she had told him to make at Berwick and took out a grey wig and a white beard and moustache which he put on, and then he smeared meal on his cheeks and hands because they were a mite young-looking.

"Aye, ye'll do fine," the lassie said, and off Jock set along the mill-lade, bent with age and limping along just as the miller did when his corns were hurting him.

It wasn't long before the king rode up with his men.

"Ye look a wee bit older than when I last saw ye," he said.

"I feel a wee bit older," the miller answered. (But you know, and I know, it wasn't the miller at all but Jock, his lad, though the king didn't know that of course.)

"Did ye find out the answers to the three questions?" the king asked.

"To tell ye the truth, I've been so busy that I clean forgot about those questions. Now, let me see – what was the first one?"

"The first one," the king said, "is what is the weight of the moon?"

"That's an easy one."

"If it's easy, then tell me the answer," the king ordered.

"Why, it's this. The moon has four quarters. Now every miller knows that four quarters make one hundredweight, so the moon weighs exactly one hundredweight." (I know you can guess who told Jock to say that!) "And if ye don't believe me," he continued, "ye can go and weigh it for yourself."

The king cleared his throat, scratched his head and turned round to look at his men, but when it became obvious that none of them had anything to·say, he cleared his throat again.

"Weel," he said, "I expect ye're right. But what about the second question?"

"The second question?"

"Aye. How many stars are there in the sky?"

"That's easier still. There are exactly one million and one."

"One million and one?" the king repeated, amazed.

"Aye. Aye, and if ye don't believe me, ye can count them tonight for yourself."

"Weel," the king said after clearing his throat, scratching his head and looking at his men, "I expect ye're right. But" – and now he couldn't keep the triumph out of his voice – "what about the third question?"

"And what was that again?"

"Tell me what I'm thinking this minute, good Master Miller."

"That's the easiest of the lot, Your Majesty. Ye think ye're talking to the old miller, but ye're not. Ye're talking to Jock, the miller's apprentice, who's soon to become the miller's son-in-law."

Straightening up, Jock removed his beard, moustache and wig and bowed to the king, and very gracefully he did it – for hadn't the miller's daughter been making him practise every evening for goodness knows how long?

The king – well, he couldn't help laughing at the way Jock had tricked him; he said he was sorry he couldn't stay for the wedding and he gave Jock a purse of golden guineas as a present, and then away he and his men rode.

As for the miller, when he heard all about it he couldn't help laughing too for, thanks to Jock, he'd kept his siller and gowd, his meal, land and mill and his daughter – and he'd got himself a fine, strong, clever son-in-law.

Jock and the miller's daughter were married the very next day and for all I know the three of them are still living happily in the millhouse on the bank of the River Tweed.

The Milk-white Doo

There was once a goodman who lived in a cottage by the Water of Liddel not far from the Scottish Border, with his wife, his son, Johnny, and his little daughter, Katie.

When his wife died suddenly, he married again, but though his second wife always spoke him fair and smiled at the children when he was by, it was a different matter when he was out at work in the fields and she was alone with the children: then she opened her mouth only to find fault or scold them and whenever she looked at them her face darkened with anger and jealousy.

"I am frightened of our new minnie," Katie whispered one day to her brother. "Although I try my best to please her, I am sure she hates me and means to do me dreadful harm."

"Do not be afraid," Johnny answered. "I am here and I promise I will look after you. If she is not kinder to you, I shall tell our father and he will send our new minnie away."

But the minnie overheard what was said and made up her mind that if anyone was to leave the cottage by the Water of Liddel, it would not be her.

The following day the goodman brought in, a fine hare he had trapped and told his wife to cook it for dinner.

Carefully she prepared the hare and put it in water in the black pot that hung over the kitchen fire, and it was not long before the whole room was filled with the most delicious smell.

"I must taste a little bit," the wife declared. And she tasted and she tasted and she tasted until she found she'd tasted all the hare away.

"Oh, dear! Whatever shall I do now?" she cried, when just at that moment Johnny returned to the cottage.

"How untidy your hair is," she scolded. "Sit down on the hearth beside me and stretch out your neck and let me comb your hair and make it tidy." And as soon as Johnny did as he was bid, she cut off his head and then chopped him up and put him in the pot.

"That smells good," the goodman said as he sat down to his dinner, but after he had begun to eat he stared at his plate.

"That looks like my Johnny's foot," he said.

"Nonsense," his wife answered. "Your eyes have been dazzled by the sunlight. Anyone can see that's a hare's foot."

But Katie looked. And said nothing.

The goodman continued eating, and then he stopped and stared again.

"That looks like my little Johnny's hand," he said.

"Nonsense," his wife answered. "Your eyes have been dazzled by the sunlight. Anyone can see it's another of the hare's feet."

But Katie looked. And said nothing.

That night, however, when her father and her minnie were asleep, she crept out of her bed and gathered all the bones from the meal together in a clean white cloth, and she buried them carefully just outside the door, with a white stone under them and a white stone over them.

70

And the bones
They grew and grew
To a milk-white doo,
That took to its wings,
And away it flew.

The dove flew up and it flew on until it came to a castle. By the castle there flowed a stream in which two women were washing fine clothes of silk and satin. Down onto a rock beside them the dove flew and very softly and very sweetly it began to sing:

Pew, pew
My minnie me slew,

whereupon the women washed more slowly.

My daddy me chew.

And they stopped washing altogether.

My sister gathered my banes
And put them between two milk-white stanes.

And now they sat back on their heels and stared at the dove on the rock.

And I grew, and I grew,
To a milk-white doo,
And I took to my wings
And away I flew.

"That was a rare song," they said. "Sing it again and we'll gie ye all these fine clothes of silk and satin."

The dove sang the song again and the women clapped their hands and gave it all the fine clothes of silk and satin, and away it flew with them.

It flew up and it flew on until it came to a wretched hovel and inside was an old man counting a pile of silver coins. Through the open door flew the dove and down onto the table and very softly and very sweetly it began to sing:

Pew, pew,
My minnie me slew,

whereupon the old man counted more slowly.

My daddy me chew.

And he stopped counting altogether.

My sister gathered my banes
And put them between two milk-white stanes.

And now he sat back in his chair and stared at the dove on the table.

And I grew, and I grew,
To a milk-white doo,
And I took to my wings
And away I flew.

"That was a rare song," he said. "Sing it again and I'll gie ye all this siller."

The dove sang the song again and the old man clapped his hands and gave it all the silver coins, and away it flew with them.

It flew up and it flew on until it came to a mill and there were two millers hard at work grinding corn. Down onto the ground the dove flew and very softly and very sweetly it began to sing:

Pew, pew,
My minnie me slew,

whereupon the millers ground more slowly.

My daddy me chew.

And they stopped grinding altogether,

73

My sister gathered my banes,
And put them between two milk-white stanes.

And now they bent down and stared at the dove on the ground.

And I grew, and I grew,
To a milk-white doo,
And I took to my wings
And away I flew.

"That was a rare song," they said. "Sing it again and we'll gie ye a fine millstane."

The dove sang the song again and the millers clapped their hands and gave it a millstone, and away it flew with the heavy stone.

It circled the mill and back it flew, and it flew and it flew, over the hovel where the old man lived, over the castle and the stream where the women had washed the fine clothes of silk and satin, and on it flew until at last it alighted on the goodman's roof top.

Down to the ground it flew to gather some pebbles and these it dropped down the chimney and into the kitchen where the father, minnie and little sister Katie were sitting.

"What made that noise?" the minnie asked sharply. "Katie, do ye step outside the door and see."

Katie went to the door, opened it and stepped outside, and immediately the dove dropped the fine clothes of silk and satin at her feet. Laughing excitedly, the little girl gathered them up and ran back into the kitchen to show her father and her minnie the fine present she had been given.

"I wonder if there is anything for me," the father said, and out he went and the dove dropped all the silver coins at his feet and they rang merrily and rolled this way and that as they glinted in the sunshine. Eagerly he picked up every one and hurried back into the kitchen to show his wife and his little daughter the fine present he had been given.

"I wonder if there is anything for me," the minnie said, and out she went.

And there was.

A millstone!

The dove dropped it right on top of her, and that was the end of her and all her wickedness. The next moment the dove disappeared and there in the doorway stood Johnny, alive and smiling; and the three of them lived together happily for many a long year after that in the cottage by the Water of Liddel not far from the Scottish Border.

The Lord's Daughter and the Seal Folk of the Farnes

Long ago there dwelt in Northumbria a warrior lord with his lady wife and his two children.

They lived in a castle perched on a high rock overlooking the grey sea, the strange island of Lindisfarne and the scattered Farnes where the sea birds nested and the Seal Folk played.

Those who traded with the people of Lindisfarne always timed their journeys across the sands so that they made their crossings in safety before the sea rushed in, encircling the island and cutting it off from the mainland, while all the fishermen avoided the Wideopens, the home of the dark-eyed Old Ones, a people left over from some almost forgotten age, whose delight it was to bring sorrow and misfortune to all who dwelt in Northumbria.

One day the warrior lord fell ill of a mysterious fever and so weak did he grow that the lady summoned to her the new nursemaid – a quiet and hard-working girl about whom little was known save that her parents had died when she was young and she had then been reared by foster parents, humble fisher folk who dwelt on Lindisfarne.

"Do you care for my son and daughter," the lady said, "and give what help you can to the steward while I tend my husband." But seeing the strange look in the girl's dark eyes, she was suddenly afraid yet knew not why.

Day and night she nursed her husband, but as the warrior lord regained his strength, so his lady lost hers, until the nursemaid sent for the boy and the girl to see their mother for the last time, while she broke the news to the lord.

"Help your mother to sip this cordial," she told the girl, but the moment she was gone, the girl, filled with mistrust, opened the shutters and dropped the flask, so that it shattered on the rocks below. When she turned back, her brother was crying and she knew that their mother was dead.

"I was tired and needed to breathe fresh air," she said when the nursemaid returned, "and the flask slipped and fell to the rocks below."

The nursemaid said nothing.

Later, when the girl went out to the rocks underneath the window, there was no sign of the shattered flask, but a cluster of sea thrift, which had nodded its purple flowers in the wind the previous day, lay withered and dead.

Now the girl feared the nursemaid just as her mother had done, but she dared not say anything, as everyone, including her father and brother, held her in high regard.

The following day the nursemaid fastened the household keys to her girdle and took over the management of the castle.

"I helped your lady and steward with the castle and your lands while you were ill," she said to the warrior lord. "Now that your lady is dead and you yourself are still weak, I shall work twice as hard."

All that year she worked with the steward, seeing that everything ran smoothly, and in spite of her many duties, she found time to care for the boy and girl. Whenever possible she rode with them to Lindisfarne, where they amused themselves on the sands and among the rock pools while she visited her foster-parents.

It was on one such visit, that the boy said to his sister, "When the nursemaid first came to the castle I thought she was very plain – almost ugly. But lately she seems to have changed somehow and now I think her the most beautiful person I have ever seen."

"She has changed," the girl agreed, "but she is not as beautiful as our mother was."

"I have almost forgotten what our mother looked like," the boy confessed. "And I think our father has forgotten too."

At that moment they heard a piteous cry from the other side of the rocky headland.

"What is that?" the girl asked, and together they hurried over the rocks and down to a sandy bay where a white seal cub lay stranded, too young and helpless to make his own way back to the sea.

"Poor little seal," the girl cried, gathering him up in her arms, and she carried him to the water's edge and watched as he swam off.

Just before she and her brother turned away, a large grey seal surfaced and appeared to watch them and then, when she was joined by her cub, both dived and were lost beneath the waves.

As they returned to the cottage where the foster-parents of their nursemaid lived, a stranger hurried out of the door, making for a light boat riding at anchor in the bay, and as he passed the boy and girl he stared at them malevolently with dark eyes that flashed beneath dark brows.

"He is one of the Old Ones from the Wideopens," the boy whispered. "Do you think he means to cause sorrow and misfortune to our nursemaid?"

At that moment the nursemaid appeared in the doorway and she looked from the man who was putting off in the boat to the girl, and her dark eyes flashed angrily beneath dark brows.

"How beautiful she is," the boy whispered, but the girl said nothing, for now she knew that their nursemaid was one of the Old Ones herself and was to cause them sorrow and misfortune.

It was not long after this that the warrior lord announced that he was to marry the nursemaid and gave orders for a great feast to be prepared to celebrate the event.

Everyone rejoiced at the news – except the girl.

At the feast she could neither eat nor drink, and in the weeks that followed she grew pale and thin, and spent hours wandering alone on the shore, gazing out to sea, watching the sea birds wheel and dive and the Seal Folk play in the cold, grey waters.

It was early one May morning, before anyone else was stirring, that the new stepmother came to the girl's room and wakened her.

"The sun is shining and it is two hours since high water," she said with a false smile. "Dress yourself while I saddle the ponies and we shall ride across to Lindisfarne, you and I, and forget the cares of the castle."

Obediently the girl rose and dressed herself and together they rode from the castle, the girl on her white pony, the stepmother on the black, and then they set off across the ridged yellow sands to the distant island.

"Surely the little pools of sea water in the yellow sands are growing and spreading all the time?" the girl said presently.

"Oh, no. It is just the early morning sun which

makes the pools sparkle and dazzles you with its light," the stepmother answered.

And on they rode.

"Surely the little streams which cross the yellow sands are becoming deeper and wider all the time?" the girl said, a little later.

"Oh, no. It is just the early morning sun which makes the streams sparkle and dazzles you with its light," the stepmother answered.

And on they rode.

"Surely the sea is making, not ebbing?" the girl cried when they came to the half way ford, and now she could see the white breakers creeping round both northern and southern ends of the island.

At this the stepmother laughed and dropped one of her embroidered gloves into the ever deepening river.

"Alas!" she cried. "That was a present to me from the warrior lord, your father, and I would not lose it for anything. You are young and nimble. Dismount and save it for me, before the little waves carry it away."

As the girl dismounted, the stepmother laughed again and called out something in a strange tongue so that the advancing waves encircled the island and crept over the yellow sands, swirling and lapping round the legs of the black pony and the white, tugging at the skirts of the girl's velvet gown and carrying the glove ever farther away.

She is a Storm Witch and is indeed one of the Old Ones, the girl thought, as the sky darkened and the waters grew deeper with every step she took.

When at last she reached the glove and turned round, it was to see her stepmother galloping back to the mainland on her black pony and leading the white beside her.

"Do not leave me here to drown," the girl cried, but

her stepmother spared her never a second glance and disappeared among the sand dunes on the shore.

"Alas! What will become of my father and brother if I do not return to warn them my stepmother is a Storm Witch?" the girl cried, struggling to make her way back to the mainland, but each step was more difficult than the last as now the waves were surging and breaking round her waist.

"Do not weep, young maiden," a voice behind her said, and turning, she saw a splendid young seal regarding her with sympathetic eyes.

"Do you not recognize the white seal cub that was stranded in the sandy bay of Lindisfarne? Then, you saved my life: now, it is my turn to save yours.

"Look at me, and take the sea light from my eyes to yours, the sea breath from my mouth to your mouth and the sea strength from my body to your own."

And the girl looked at the young seal, and took the sea light from his eyes to hers, so that she could see beneath the waves, the sea breath from his mouth to her mouth so that she could breathe under water, and the sea strength from his body to her own so that she could swim for long distances without surfacing, just as the seals can.

"Now follow me," he said, and he led her under the waves past the island of Lindisfarne and the Inner Farnes where dwelt the fisher folk, past the Wide-opens which belonged to the terrible Old Ones, and far out to sea to a magnificent palace of fretted coral and mother of pearl, which was the home of the Seal Folk.

There the girl was welcomed by the Seal Queen herself, and there she learned that the cub she had rescued and who, in turn, had rescued her, was the Seal Prince, loved and admired by all the Seal Folk.

The prince soon taught her to speak his language, and entertained her with tales of his forefathers who had lived off the coast of Northumbria centuries before.

The days passed and the weeks, until the time came when the girl suddenly remembered her father and her brother whom she had loved so dearly. So sad and silent did she grow that the prince asked her at length why she no longer laughed and sang as she had learned to do since she came to live with them.

"Although you are all very good and kind to me," she answered, "I cannot help missing my father and my brother, and dearly would I like to return for just one day to satisfy myself they are well and happy."

"Wait with us a little longer," the queen begged, "and I shall find out what news there is of your father and brother."

Rising to the surface, she called out to a passing fulmar, and immediately the great grey and white bird wheeled and returned to the coast and questioned one of his cousins there.

"The warrior lord is well enough," he reported the following day, "and his son is happy enough but mourns for his sister who he thinks was drowned. All the old servants and retainers at the castle have been dismissed and replaced by others of the stepmother's choice."

"The time has not yet come for you to return," the queen said, when she heard this. "Be advised by me and stay with us a little longer."

Swimming and diving and listening to the tales the prince told of his forefathers who had lived off the Western Islands of Scotland, the girl lived happily beneath the sea, until the time came again when she remembered her father and brother and wished to return for just one day to satisfy herself that they were well and happy.

This time the queen called out to a guillemot who was diving for fish and the big, white-breasted bird immediately rose and made for the coast and questioned her relatives there.

"The warrior lord is well enough," she reported the following day, "but the son has a mind to be a sailor and will not be content until he gets his way. The steward has been dismissed and the farmers and fishermen have been turned out of their homes and been replaced by others of the stepmother's choice."

"The time has not yet come for you to return," the queen said when she heard this. "Be advised by me and stay with us a little longer."

Swimming and diving and listening to the tales the prince told of his forefathers who lived off the Islands of Orkney and Shetland, the girl lived happily beneath the sea until the time came again when she remembered her father and brother and wished to return for just one day to make sure they were well and happy.

This time the queen called out to a storm petrel who was following a ship and the little, black ocean bird immediately rose and made for the coast and questioned his relatives there.

"The warrior lord sits sad and melancholy by his fireside," he reported the following day, "and the brother has sailed for foreign parts and will not return for a year and a day. The stepmother fills the castle with friends of her own choice and every week there is feasting and dancing and merrymaking."

"When your brother returns, that will be the time for you to go back to your land," the queen said. "Content yourself and stay with us a little longer."

The girl contented herself until a year and a day had

passed, when shoals of fish swam down to the bed of the ocean and the palace of the Seal Folk.

"The sky is black with storm clouds," they reported. "Great breakers rear and crash on the troubled seas and gales whip high in the air the torn spindrift. All the seabirds have sought safety on ledges and crevices in the rocks or have flown inland to the lakes and ponds and streams.

"We are sorry for the sailors on the ship with torn sails that even now is tossed like a cork towards the rocks of Lindisfarne. One thing is sure – the ship will founder in a few minutes."

"Poor sailors," the girl cried, weeping because she knew there was nothing she or the Seal Folk could do to help those in such danger.

"This is no ordinary storm," said the Seal Queen. "This has been conjured up by your stepmother, whom we all know to be a Storm Witch, and a daughter of one of the terrible Old Ones left over from an almost forgotten age."

At this, the girl shivered and drew near to the seals, grateful for the home they had given her and the protection they had afforded her.

When she awoke the next day, she rose to the surface of the sea with the seals, to find the storm had blown itself out and the sun was shining, but the ship with torn sails had foundered on the cruel rocks and the wreckage was strewn along the shores of Lindisfarne.

Sadly the girl walked among the debris on the sand, until she came to a young sailor who lay in the sunshine as though he were sleeping, but when she stooped to waken him, the Seal Queen stopped her.

"The sea has claimed him," she said. "This is the work of the Storm Witch, your stepmother." And when the girl looked down again she saw that the sailor was her own brother.

"Is there nothing you can do to restore him to me?" she asked.

"My son and my people have come to love you dearly," the queen answered. "If I restore your brother to life, would you stay with us for ever?"

The girl stared across Lindisfarne to the yellow sands and green fields of Northumbria and the distant castle that was her home, and then she looked down at her brother.

"Restore him to life and I will stay with you," she promised.

Around her the seals moaned softly, as though each of them felt her grief.

"We could never keep you with us against your desire," the queen said gently. "But because you have been kind and patient and loving all the time you have lived with us, your brother shall be restored to life and you shall both return to your home.

"Take this silver flask which contains the most precious healing liquid known to the Seal Folk. Wait until we have taken our farewell of you and swum down to the ocean bed, and then let one drop fall on each of his eyelids, each of his nostrils and each of his lips, and your brother will arise as though he had just been sleeping.

"Go back to your castle and let the drops fall again on the eyes, nostrils and lips of your brother, your father and on you too, and you will see that the magic of the Seal Folk is greater than that of the Storm Witch and the terrible Old Ones."

Thanking the queen for the precious gift, the girl took the flask.

"Because of all you have done for me," she said, "I

promise that no harm shall ever come to any of you from me or my family or those who work for us, and I promise that from now Lindisfarne and the Farne Islands will always be safe for you and your children."

Sadly she watched as they disappeared, one by one, beneath the waves, until only the prince remained, and as she gave back to him the sea light, the sea breath and the sea strength, his eyes were full of sorrow because he had loved her so faithfully and so long and now knew that he must lose her.

For a long time the girl wept at the loss of the prince and all the Seal Folk, and then at last she unstoppered the flask and let fall the drops, and as the sixth drop touched her brother's lower lip, he sprang up and stared at her in amazement for he thought she had been drowned long ago.

Hand in hand they walked across the ribbed sands, talking of all that had happened since they had parted.

When they reached the shore of Northumbria they saw with dismay how neglected and overgrown were the fields and pastures, how the doors of the cottages were closed and the windows shuttered, and they were saddened because there was no sound of women singing at their spinning wheels nor any laughter of children at play.

As they climbed up to the castle, however, they heard shouting and laughter and strange, wild music, and when they entered the great hall they passed unnoticed through crowds of handsome young men and lovely ladies who were feasting and drinking. But the loveliest lady of all was their stepmother.

"Do not stare at her so," the girl said, and she led her brother to the fire where an old man sat, his clothing torn and dirty, his beard and hair white and neglected.

Gently she spoke to the old man, and when he looked up and did not recognize her, she unstoppered the flask and placed six drops on his face, and on her brother's and on her own, as the Seal Queen had told her. Immediately her father yawned, stretched and rose to his feet, tall and strong and a warrior lord again.

"What is happening in my castle?" he demanded, and turning, the girl and her brother saw that instead of handsome young men and lovely ladies, the hall was full of geese and toads, snakes, cockroaches and slugs, and in place of their beautiful stepmother, there crouched an ugly, old hag.

"Away with you!" the warrior lord shouted in a terrible voice as he flung open the castle doors. At the sound of these words the stepmother shrieked and she and the loathsome creatures crumbled slowly away to dust which the salt wind scattered far over the grey sea.

Now that the spell was lifted the girl fastened the household keys to her girdle and took over the management of the castle, and the warrior lord sent for his steward and retainers and for all the farmers and fishermen the stepmother had turned out of their homes, and everyone set to work with a will so that soon they were as happy and prosperous as before, and once again there was the sound of women singing and children laughing as they played on the yellow sands.

And sometimes, of a moonlit night, the girl would slip down to the seashore and call softly to the seals in their own language – for that was one gift she had been allowed to keep – and the Seal Queen and the prince and the other Seal People would swim to her feet and talk to her of all they had seen and done.

When eventually the girl married the son of a neighbouring lord and had children of her own, the Seal Folk taught them how to dive and swim, to know and avoid the dangerous currents and reefs, and to tell the speed of the making and ebbing seas between Lindisfarne and the mainland.

So they lived happily together for a long, long time, and to this day the Seal Folk live in peace on the Farne Islands and swim and play in the cold, grey sea.

The Laddie who kept Hares

Once there was a poor widow with two fine, strong sons. They lived in a wee cottage close by the Happertutie Burn, which trickles into Yarrow Water before it flows into St. Mary's Loch.

Times were hard. There was little work for the sons and less to eat, and at last the elder son announced that he was of a mind to go out into the world and seek his fortune.

"What must be, must be," the widow said, and gave her son a sieve and a cracked bowl from the kitchen table. "Away with ye down to the well and bring me back some water. The more water ye fetch home, the bigger the bannock I'll bake for ye."

Off the elder son went with the sieve and the cracked bowl to the well by the steep, sloping bank of the Happertutie Burn, and there on a briar bush among the reeds and marsh marigolds, what did he see but a bonnie wee birdie singing to the blue sky above.

The moment the wee birdie saw the elder son with the sieve in one hand and the cracked bowl in the other, he changed his song.

> Stop it wi' fog and clag it wi' clay,
> And that'll carry the water away.

"Ye stupid creature!" the elder son cried angrily. "Who do ye think ye are to be giving advice to a fine, strong young man like me? Do ye think I'll dirty my hands with moss and clay just because ye tell me to?

90

Away with ye and leave me in peace to do things my own way."

He watched as the wee birdie flew off and then turned to the well. Of course the water ran out of the sieve as fast as he tried to fill it, nor was he any more successful with the cracked bowl, so that in the end he returned with only a few drops in the bottom of the bowl and none at all in the sieve.

On seeing this the widow sighed, and then set to work and baked a wee, wee bannock with oatmeal and the few drops of water, and off the elder son set to seek his fortune: in so much of a hurry was he that he had time neither to bid his younger brother good-bye nor to ask for his mother's blessing.

On he walked and on, as far as I can tell you or you can tell me, through birks and brakes and over the hills of Yarrow and at last, wearied out, he sat down under a birch tree to eat his wee, wee bannock.

Before he had time to take the first bite, the bonnie wee birdie flew down and settled on a birk branch beside him.

"Give me a bite of your wee, wee bannock and I'll give ye one of my wing feathers so ye can fashion a pair of pipes for yourself," he said.

"Ye stupid creature!" the elder son cried angrily. "What do I want with a pair of pipes when I'm away to seek my fortune? It's all your fault that I have such a wee, wee bannock: there's hardly enough for me and there's certainly not enough to waste on ye. Away with ye and bad luck to ye."

Away the wee birdie flew without another word, while the elder son ate his bannock greedily and then set off again.

On he walked and on, as far as I can tell you or you can tell me, through birks and brakes and over the hills of Yarrow, until at last he came to a house where a king lived.

This is the place for me, he said to himself, and in he walked and asked if there was any work for a fine, strong young man.

"What can ye do?" the king asked.

"I can sweep the floor, carry out the ashes each morning and keep the cattle."

"Can ye keep hares?" the king asked.

Well, the elder brother knew all about watching over cattle and sheep to make sure they didn't stray, but he'd never heard of anyone watching over hares, but if that was the only work there was, then, he decided, he was the man for it.

"Aye. I can keep hares."

"Good," the king said, rubbing his hands together. "Tomorrow ye'll have my hares to keep. If ye bring them all back safely here at night ye can marry my daughter."

"That suits me," the elder brother said, rubbing his hands together as he thought how quickly and easily he was going to make his fortune and marry a princess into the bargain.

"But if ye don't bring them all back safely," the king added, "I'll have to hang ye."

The elder brother didn't like the sound of that a bit, but as there was nothing he could do about it now and as the king didn't say anything about supper, he went to bed and slept soundly.

The next morning when he went downstairs the king was just finishing his breakfast: he'd eaten all the porridge and all the bannocks and drunk all the ale, and there was only a cup of water left for the elder brother.

"When ye've drunk that up," he said, "go down to

the Auld Dyke Field, where my hares are playing. Keep them and bring them safely back here tonight."

The elder brother drank the water and off he went, and when he reached the Auld Dyke field, there he saw four and twenty hares and one wee lame one playing in the long green grass.

Down he sat and started grumbling to himself because he had had nothing to eat that morning and only a wee, wee bannock the day before, and that, he thought, was no way to treat a hero who was going to marry a king's daughter.

So up he got and chased the hares and soon he caught the wee, lame one, which he skinned and roasted and ate. After that he went to sleep.

When he woke up the sun was westering and so he set about trying to catch the four and twenty hares, but they had seen what had happened to the wee lame one and they didn't like him a bit and scurried away as fast as they could in different directions, so that although he chased after them and called and shouted and whistled until the sun had set and it was quite dark, not one of the hares did he succeed in catching.

When at last he returned to the house, the king was waiting for him.

"Did ye keep the hares?" he asked.

"I would have done, but they all ran away."

"Even the wee lame one?"

"I ate it because I was hungry."

"Take him away and hang him," the king cried angrily.

And that, I'm afraid, was the end of the elder brother.

Twelve months after the elder brother had left the cottage close by the Happertutie Burn, the younger brother told his mother that he was of a mind to go out into the world and seek his fortune.

"What must be, must be," the widow said, and she gave the laddie a sieve and a cracked bowl from the kitchen table. "Away with ye down to the well and bring me back some water. The more water ye fetch home, the bigger the bannock I'll bake for ye."

Off the laddie went with the sieve and the cracked bowl to the well by the steep, sloping bank of the Happertutie Burn, and there on a briar bush among the reeds and marsh marigolds, what did he see but a bonnie wee birdie singing to the blue sky above.

The moment the wee birdie saw the laddie with the sieve in one hand and the cracked bowl in the other, he changed his song.

> Stop it wi' fog and clag it wi' clay,
> And that'll carry the water away.

"Thank ye, my bonnie wee birdie," the laddie said and he set to work and lined the sieve and the cracked bowl with damp moss and then he smoothed clay over the moss so that both were watertight; finally he filled each from the well and carried them carefully home to his mother.

On seeing this the widow was well pleased and immediately set to work and baked a fine, big bannock with oatmeal and water.

"Give me your blessing with the bannock," the laddie said, and his mother blessed him and sighed and then smiled as she watched him go.

On he walked and on, as far as I can tell you or you can tell me, through birks and brakes and over the hills of Yarrow and at last, wearied out, he sat down under a birch tree and took out his fine, big bannock.

Before he had time to break off one piece, the bonnie

wee birdie flew down and settled on a birk branch beside him.

"Give me a bite of your fine big bannock and I'll give ye one of my wing feathers so ye can fashion a pair of pipes for yourself," he said.

"Ye're welcome to all ye can eat, my bonnie wee birdie, for it was ye who told me to stop the sieve and the bowl with fog and clag it with clay so that I could carry the water back to my mother." He broke off a piece and gave it to the wee birdie and then he divided the rest in two and half he put in his pocket and the other half he ate.

"That was grand," the wee birdie said, when he had pecked up every crumb. "Now pull a feather from my wing and fashion yourself a pair of pipes."

"Och, I can't do a thing like that," the laddie protested. "If I pulled out a feather it would hurt ye."

"No, no, that it won't. Just ye do what I tell ye. Pull out one of my wing feathers and fashion it into a pair of pipes."

Reluctantly the laddie pulled out a feather, surprised to find how easily it came away, and then he watched as the bonnie wee birdie soared singing into the bright blue sky and was lost in the sunlight.

At length he took out his knife, and very carefully he trimmed off the soft barbs: the quill and the shaft he cut into two and notched, and when he had fashioned his pipes he raised them to his lips, and the tune he played was the song of the bonnie wee birdie as it had soared into the sky.

Now instead of walking the laddie danced to the magic tune of his pipes: on he danced and on, as far as I can tell you or you can tell me, through birks and brakes and over the hills of Yarrow until at last he came to the house where the king lived.

Perhaps this is the place for me, he said to himself, and in he walked and asked if there was any work for a willing young laddie.

"What can ye do?" the king asked.

"I can sweep the floor, carry out the ashes each morning and keep the cattle."

"Can ye keep hares?" the king asked.

The laddie thought it over.

"I can try," he said at last.

"Good." The king rubbed his hands together. "Tomorrow ye'll have my hares to keep. If ye bring them all back safely here at night ye can marry my daughter."

"That suits me," the laddie said, "as long as it suits her."

"Ye think about yourself and I'll think about my daughter," the king said sharply. "Just mind that if ye don't bring all my hares back safely, I'll have to hang ye."

The laddie didn't like the sound of that a bit, but as there was nothing he could do about it now and as the king didn't say anything about supper, he went to his room, took out what was left of the fine big bannock his mother had given him that morning, broke it in two and after eating one half, fell fast asleep.

The next morning when he went downstairs the king was just finishing his breakfast: he'd eaten all the porridge and all the bannocks and drunk all the ale, and there was only a cup of water left for the laddie.

"When ye've drunk that up," he said, "go down to the Auld Dyke Field where my hares are playing. Keep them and bring them safely back here tonight."

Off the laddie went without a word and when he came to the Auld Dyke Field he saw the four and twenty hares and the one wee lame one playing happily in the long green grass: sitting down to watch over them he took out the last piece of his mother's fine, big bannock and ate it slowly until not a single crumb was left.

And then he took out his pipes and began to play, so bonnie, bonnie that the hares left off their games and looked at him and then began to dance, drawing nearer and nearer until they formed a circle round him and he in the middle and the pipe music so bonnie, bonnie filling all the air.

Everywhere now there was the magic stillness of peace: the fish in the river nearby lay at rest, the water fowl drowsed among the reeds, the field creatures slumbered in the shade, the dragonflies poised motionless on the yellow gowans and the kingfisher dreamed on the branch of a birk tree.

Only the hares moved.

All day they danced and not until the sun was westering did the laddie stop piping, and then the fish and the water fowl, the field creatures and the dragonflies and the kingfisher stirred again at the very moment that the hares stopped dancing.

"Now we must go home," the laddie said.

He turned towards the house and the four and twenty hares began to follow him. But the wee lame one was too tired to walk and lay down in the long green grass.

"The strong must help the weak," the laddie said, and he picked up the wee lame hare and carried her in his arms and stroked her head, and when he looked down at her big brown eyes he thought they were the most beautiful he had ever seen.

When he returned to the house he took the four and twenty hares to their barn for the night, but the wee lame one he took to his room and placed gently on his bed and then went downstairs.

"Did ye keep the hares?" the king asked.

"Aye, I did that."

"Where are they?"

The laddie went to the barn, opened the door and the four and twenty hares leaped out and into the house.

"What about the wee lame one?"

"I carried her back and put her on my bed."

"Go and fetch her to me."

The laddie went to his room but instead of a wee lame hare there sat a princess with long hair and the most beautiful big brown brown eyes he had ever seen.

"It seems that ye have lost a hare but found my daughter," the king said, well pleased. "Ye shall be married tomorrow."

"That suits me," the laddie said, "as long as it suits your daughter."

The princess said that she thought it would suit her, but she'd like a little time to think it over.

"Perhaps some music would help?" the laddie suggested, seeing the king scowling angrily; and he put his pipes to his lips and the house was filled with the magic tune the laddie had learned from the bonnie wee birdie as it had soared into the bright blue sky. At once all work was stopped and everyone began to dance – the maids and the menservants, the four and twenty hares and the princess and even the king himself: the livelong night they danced and laughed and laughed and danced, and when the sun rose the next morning the princess announced that now she had had time to think it over and she was sure the laddie would suit her fine.

The king at once sent for the laddie's mother and gave her a cottage of her own near his house. As for the laddie and the princess, they had a fine wedding and guests came to it from Ettrick and Tweed and Yarrow, and when the king died, the laddie ruled in his stead.

The Cowt of Kielder and the Wicked Lord Soulis

Long, long ago, when there was magic black and white in the land and wizards and hobgoblins too, there lived a young chieftain in a castle on the south bank of the Kielder Burn, which flows into the River North Tyne.

He was handsome and brave, reckless and daring, and so renowned for his great size and strength that throughout the English and Scottish Borderlands he was called the Cowt – or Colt – of Kielder.

Now the Cowt had a lady mother who was well versed in magic and who was resolved that her son should have all the protection possible against his enemies, whether they were other men or creatures left over from an earlier age. She arranged therefore, for a mermaid – whose life she had saved when some Berwick fishermen had caught her in their net and were about to kill her – to fashion her son a helmet of magic sand.

To this helmet the lady mother added two ostrich plumes – brought from the far East and possessed of a strange magic – and holly and rowan leaves, which, as everyone knows to this day, have the power of warding off all evil.

The man whom the lady mother feared most was Sir William Soulis, Lord of Liddesdale, who lived on the far side of the Border, in Hermitage Castle, in Scotland. And the creature she most dreaded was the

Brown Man of the Moors, a hobgoblin who delighted in wickedness and who was known to be an ally and accomplice of Lord Soulis, the wizard and dealer in black magic.

Whenever she tried to warn her son against these two, the Cowt only laughed.

"Thanks to my helmet, I am a match and more than a match for any man or hobgoblin," he insisted and he paid but little heed to the many tales that were told of the wicked Lord Soulis.

It was one fine Spring day, when the Cowt and his men were practising archery in the grounds of Kielder Castle, that a messenger came from across the Border.

"My Lord Soulis bade me say that the time has come when all old quarrels between Hermitage and Kielder should be forgotten, and to that end he invites the Cowt and his men to join him tomorrow in a day of hunting, to be followed by a splendid feast."

"Do not go, my son," the lady mother begged. "Everyone knows that Lord Soulis is not to be trusted. For long his family has hated ours and no matter what he says, he is jealous of you and means you ill."

The Cowt frowned.

"Would you have Lord Soulis and his Scots think me a coward that I dare not hunt and feast with them?" he demanded.

"Then wear your magic casque of sand with the holly green and leaves from the rowan tree," his lady mother begged.

"That I shall do most willingly," the Cowt answered.

"And do not ride widdershins round the Kielder Stone as so often you do, for that can only bring ill luck."

"Nay, I am no child to be told that I must do this and

I must not do that," the Cowt protested with a frown, and as his men obviously agreed with their young chieftain, his lady mother said no more but turned and walked back to the castle. Before she had reached the door a black magpie flew across her path and then she knew she had good reason to be afraid, as the sight of one such bird meant certain death.

The following morning she tried again to persuade her son to refuse the invitation, but again he laughed at her fears and said she must have the same faith in his magic helmet as he had.

Out of the castle gates they rode, the Cowt and his men and hounds and as was usual when they were crossing into Scotland – whether on friendly business or on a raid to replenish their larders – they made straight for the Kielder Stone, a massive, jagged rock which lay on the Border line, half in England and half in Scotland.

"Perhaps your lady mother was right, and it might bring ill luck to ride widdershins round the rock," one of his men said. He had been discussing the matter with his wife the previous evening and she had told him, in no uncertain terms, how unwise it was to court bad luck.

"Riding contrary to the way of the sun is inviting disaster," another agreed: he too had been roundly scolded by his mother for his foolhardiness.

An outburst of shrill laughter behind them startled the Cowt and his men and set the hounds barking furiously as they tried to slip their leashes. Turning in his saddle, the Cowt saw the Brown Man of the Moors grinning malevolently up at him.

"So the great and valiant and fearless Cowt of Kielder is afraid to ride three times widdershins round the Kielder Stone, is he?" he cried mockingly. "That will be a tale to entertain the Scots with tonight, and for many a long night afterwards."

"Afraid?" the Cowt repeated, growing red with anger. "No man dare say I am afraid of anything – and live. And no hobgoblin, either." And drawing his sword, which flashed in the sunlight, he laughed to see the Brown Man skip out of reach, fear in his eyes. "I have a mind to separate your head from your shoulders, little man," he cried.

"Sheathe your sword, young Cowt," the Brown Man answered. "I am protected by magic, just as you are. But to prove your courage, forget those old wives' tales and ride thrice round the Kielder Stone – widdershins."

Without a word the Cowt sheathed his sword, and his men fell silent, eyeing one another uneasily, while the hounds made no sound at all. Spurring on his horse, three times the young chieftain rode round the Stone, each time contrary to the way of the sun, and then his men, still uneasy but unwilling to be outdone, each in turn rode three times widdershins round the Kielder Stone.

As the last man reined his horse to a halt the Brown Man laughed mockingly and disappeared so quickly that no one had any idea in which direction he had gone. At the same moment a dark cloud hid the sun and the leader of the hounds lifted his head and bayed mournfully, and now the men avoided one another's glances, suddenly afraid but not knowing what it was they had to fear.

"Come, lads! To Liddesdale and the hunt!" the Cowt shouted.

"To Liddesdale and the hunt!" the men answered, calling on their courage and reminding themselves of the excitement of the chase, while at the back of their

minds they drew strength from the memory of raids in which they had fought and brave deeds they had performed.

"To Liddesdale and the hunt!" a faint voice called mockingly, and though they could not see him, they knew the Brown Man of the Moors was watching and even now might know what fate was in store for them.

Over tussocks of coarse grass and heather, round peat hags and bogland the Cowt led his men, skirting the mass of Peel Fell and passing the lonely Wheel Kirk where Scots and English met to settle their quarrels: down Liddesdale they rode to where the great, grey castle of Hermitage stood on the green bank of the Hermitage Water, which some men call the Marching Burn, and there Lord Soulis and his retainers and his hounds awaited them.

"This is an historic occasion," Lord Soulis cried, in welcoming tones. "On this fair day when Hermitage and Kielder hunt together we shall have such sport as each man here will remember to the last day of his life, and tonight there will be such feasting and drinking as will be remembered throughout the whole of the brave Borderland."

All day they hunted, Scots and Englishmen together, and in the excitement and dangers of the chase it seemed to the Cowt and his men that old quarrels were forgotten and new friendships forged. Finally, flushed with triumph at the sight of the animals they had so nobly killed, they returned to Hermitage and there sat down to a feast of roast venison, boar's head, mutton pies, pigeons' eggs, stuffed capons, broiled ptarmigan, grouse and hare pie, and all kinds of sweetmeats, with copious flagons of ale and wine from France. At the same time the Cowt's hounds mixed with those of Lord Soulis and shared the food thrown to them on the floor.

But Lord Soulis had read deep in his books of poison and had made full use of his knowledge of herbs of evil humours: to the dishes served to the Cowt and his men were added the juices of deadly nightshade and other plants of ill repute, so that presently the Cowt perceived that his men sat as though carved from stone, transfixed in their seats in the act of eating or drinking or laughing, while his hounds were lying, motionless on the floor.

"Traitor!" he cried, leaping back from his stool, sword in one hand, dagger in the other. "You may have cast your evil spell on my men, but never can you hope to kill me.

"In my plume is seen the holly green,
With the leaves of the rowan tree;
And my casque of sand by a mermaid's hand
Was formed beneath the sea."

With lightning play he took on and killed first one of Lord Soulis' men and then another.

"What would you give to know the flaw in the charm that protects the young Cowt?" a shrill voice asked, and Lord Soulis looked down to find the Brown Man of the Moors at his elbow.

"A chest filled to the very top with coins of gold," the wicked lord answered, seeing yet another of his retainers fall beneath the Cowt's deadly blade.

"His life is charmed on land, but the charm avails not in water. Drive him out of doors and down to the burn and then he will be at your mercy."

Already, however, fighting valiantly all the time, the Cowt was retreating step by step from the castle, hoping to ford the burn and escape on his horse, and though many attacked him and many were slain, no sword penetrated his armour or so much as scratched his skin.

Just as he reached the banks of the burn, he stumbled and fell backwards into a deep pool.

"Hold him down!" Lord Soulis shouted, and his retainers caught the Cowt with their spears and held him down so that his struggles were all in vain.

> The holly floated to the tide
> And the leaf of the rowan pale;
> Alas! no spell could charm the tide
> Nor the lance of Liddesdale.

> Swift was the Cowt of Kielder's course
> Along the lily lee;
> But home came never hound nor horse
> And never home came he.

And ever since that day, the place where the young chieftain was drowned has been called the Cowt of Kielder's Pool.

When his lady mother heard what had happened she dressed herself all in black, and, covering her face with a black veil, she sent for her seven brothers and their men.

"My magic availed me nought, and now the Cowt of Kielder lies dead on the banks of the Marching Burn.

"Of all the places dear to my son in this fair North Country, most of all he loved the Bell's Burn which flows into the River Tyne near its source. Carry him there, I beg of you, and bury him by the Kirk o' Bells."

Her brothers and their men did as the lady mother asked, and they carried the Cowt to the Kirk o' Bells – which is but a tumbled heap of stones today – and the place where he was buried is called the Cowt's Grave, and is marked by two large, grey stones, which were placed one at his head and the other at his feet.

> *This is the bonny brae, the green*
> *Yet sacred to the brave,*
> *Where still, of ancient size, is seen*
> *Gigantic Kielder's grave.*

But the Cowt's lady mother, and the wives and mothers of the retainers who sat for ever in a magic trance in the vaults of Hermitage Castle, were but a few of the many people Lord Soulis had harmed, and now all those who had been injured by him in any way called on the King of Scotland to protect them from such an evil man. Even his own followers joined in the outcry, declaring that so great was the wickedness committed in Hermitage, that the castle had already sunk one foot into the ground!

The king, it is said, growing weary of hearing all the reports of the evil deeds of Lord Soulis, turned to his soldiers and cried, "Ride down to Hermitage and rid me and my kingdom of this villain!"

"But how?" his soldiers demanded, knowing that Soulis was a wizard and could not be killed by any mortal man.

"What would you give to know how to undo the charm that protects Lord Soulis?" a shrill voice asked and, looking down, the King saw the Brown Man of the Moors at his elbow.

"A chest filled to the very top with precious stones," he answered.

"Bend down, O King, that I may whisper in your ear," the Brown Man of the Moors commanded, and the King bent down.

And listened.

And grew pale.

After a moment's hesitation he gave an order to the captain of his guards. Straightaway they marched to Liddesdale – captain, guards and all those whose men had been killed or injured or harmed in any way by the wicked Lord Soulis – and when they reached the Nine Stane Rig, which lies to the east of Hermitage, they built a fire and filled a huge cauldron with water from the burn and put it over the fire. And then they advanced on the castle.

"Save me! Save me!" Lord Soulis cried as the great army of soldiers and men and women burst open the castle doors. But there was no one – man, woman or child – who did not hate him for his cruelty, his avarice and his treachery, and there was no one to come to his aid as he was dragged, shrieking, to the top of the rigg.

They rolled him up in a sheet of lead,
A sheet of lead for a funeral pall;
They plunged him in the cauldron red,
And melted him – lead and bones and all.

The brown Man of the Moors laughed shrilly when he heard what had happened, and on his back he carried the chest of precious stones, making across the moors for the underground dwelling where he lived and where his chest filled with coins of gold was already hidden. But the lady mother of the Cowt of Kielder marked his progress in her magic mirror, and calling on her secret powers she conjured up a great black heaving bog in front of the hurrying hobgoblin and before he realized what was happening, he was sucked down and down and down: and from that day to this nothing more was ever heard of him and no one has ever found either his chest of gold coins or his chest of precious stones.

Once, so people said, you could see for yourself the great cauldron in which the wicked Lord Soulis met his doom, but one dark night it disappeared and was never seen again.

The ruins of Hermitage Castle still stand, sad and proud but peaceful now, on the green bank of the Hermitage Water that was once called the Marching Burn, in Liddesdale. As for the Kielder Stone, it still lies on the Border Line, half in England and half in Scotland, but what would happen today if you rode thrice round it widdershins no one knows – or perhaps no one dares tell.

The Witch of Rubers Law

A long time ago there lived a poor shepherd and his daughter on the far bank of the Rule Water, near the great hill of Rubers Law, in the Lowlands of Scotland.

Each year the shepherd hoped that somehow he would make just a little more money so that he could buy his daughter a new dress instead of the old patched ones she had to wear: each year the lassie gathered scraps of wool from the brambles and whins, hoping that somehow she would have enough to weave her father a fine warm plaid to replace the worn garment that no longer kept out the driving rain of winter, the bitter winds and the sleet and the snow. But though they both worked from morn till night, they made only enough to feed themselves and their animals, and though the lassie wove many a length of warm woollen cloth, she knew her father would have to take it all to the market at Hawick, to exchange it for salt and sugar and such food as they themselves could not produce.

Although they went to the Kirk every Sunday they, like the rest of the congregation, were well aware that people of a race far older than theirs still dwelt in the land: they were particularly careful not to offend the Fairy People who lived in the heart of Rubers Law, and nothing would have induced them to skirt the great hill by night, when the little people held their revels and when their magic music might lure unsuspecting travellers — and even local men who had celebrated too freely at some wedding or funeral or fair day – so that they were never seen again. Except for one man.

In spite of all his two companions could say, he had followed the music into the hillside, and though his relations searched for him for weeks, all that they found was his woollen cap lying among the bracken. Time passed. Those who had known him died and then one morning, when his great grandson was crossing Rubers Law, he came across a young stranger who somehow seemed vaguely familiar.

"Who are you and where are you going?" he asked.

"I am Tam Scott who went dancing last night and am now on my way home." But even as the stranger spoke he grew old and white and bent and as he finished the last word, he crumpled up and there was only a little pile of dust where he had stood.

Just as the shepherd and his daughter avoided Rubers Law by night, so they never visited the witch who lived with her black cat in the tumbledown cottage on the green flank of the hill. They knew, of course, that many country people – and others from as far away as Hawick – went to her for love potions and charms, to ask what the future held for them, even, so some said, for the means to ill-wish and bring trouble and bad luck to their enemies.

All this the shepherd and his daughter knew: a witch, however, they decided was different from the Fairy People, even though she was in league with them and could cause just as much trouble. But, they thought, she was an old woman without any relatives to care for her and she had to live. It was as well that some people wanted her help, the shepherd said, and were willing to pay for it in butter and eggs, cheese, cakes and sometimes a whole, fine fleece.

Although they had no need of the help of the Witch of Rubers Law, both the shepherd and the lassie greeted her pleasantly if they met her out gathering her roots and herbs and plants and on occasion, when the dreaded north-easterlies scoured the countryside or the snow lay deep and dangerous, the shepherd would fight his way over to the tumbledown cottage with peat and kindling from his own store and oatcakes of the lassie's baking, and these he would place on the step, knock three times and return home, knowing that the witch would not go cold and hungry.

One evening, just after the three 'borrowing days' which January had lent to February and which had been particularly wild and stormy, the shepherd and his daughter sat talking in front of the fire.

"Although I am glad not to hear the howl of the wind in the chimney," the shepherd said, "the severe weather of the last days is a good omen. The year ahead will be lucky for everyone."

The next morning, as the lassie picked up her father's plaid to place it over his shoulder, she was delighted to see a little spider run down it; well did she know that this meant that within the year the old garment would be replaced by a new one, and who should collect the wool and do the carding and spinning and weaving but herself?

All went well as the weeks passed. The rain came just when it was needed and the sun shone more often than the shepherd could remember; the crops grew, the animals flourished and the lassie added daily to her store of wool tufts.

It was just before Midsummer's Day, as the lassie was returning with fresh water from the river, that she looked as usual at the tumbledown cottage on the flank of Rubers Law and wondered if anything was wrong. At length she spoke to her father.

'For three days when I have gone down for water I

have looked across to Rubers Law and the door of the witch's cottage has always been closed – closed in summer, with the sun shining. And there has been no smoke from the chimney."

"She may have gone away to visit some old friend, or some relative we know nothing of," the shepherd suggested, but the lassie shook her head.

"Everyone knows she has neither kith nor kin. And in fine weather such as this she always sits at the cottage door spinning or working with the plants she has gathered. You yourself have often seen her."

"Many people call on her for help; if there was anything wrong with her, someone would have found out by now."

"Twice I have seen women knock on the door and then hurry away when it was not opened. It is true that many seek her help, but they are all frightened of her and dare not set foot inside her cottage."

"I am not sure that I am not frightened of her myself," the shepherd confessed, "but I cannot leave an old woman in distress any more than I could a new-born lamb. Tomorrow morning, if the door is not open or the chimney smoking, I shall go and see for myself if there is anything wrong and I shall take some peat and kindling with me so that the witch will not think me curious or interfering."

"And I shall come with you, Father, and take some of my buttermilk scones and a black pudding too."

The next morning the door was still closed, the window was shuttered and there was no smoke from the chimney. Again and again the shepherd knocked on the door, but the only sound he could hear inside was the plaintive miaowing of a cat.

"If it is only to let out the cat I must break in the door," the shepherd said, and putting his shoulder to the warped wood he broke the latch which held the bar in place on the inside. As the door swung open, the black cat darted out and downhill to the river, but the witch lay still and silent on the earthen floor.

"Is she dead?" the lassie asked, as her father knelt down.

"No," he said at length. "I think she fell some little time ago and hit her head here, and her arm here. One thing is certain – she is in need of help, and we, who have never been beholden to her, must give it."

Together they lifted the witch onto her bed, revived her with cold water from the river, bathed her hands and face, and while the shepherd lit the fire and mended the latch he had broken, the lassie brought thin porridge made with goat's milk and sweetened with wild honey and she fed the old woman with the meal she had prepared for their own supper.

Twice a day the shepherd came to tend the fire and twice a day the lassie came and fed the witch and put down milk for the black cat, and though the old woman watched every movement with dark, glittering eyes, never a word did she speak.

On the seventh morning, however, when they arrived at the cottage the door was open and the witch was sitting just inside, spinning wool into a fine, even yarn.

"Can you weave?" she asked the lassie.

"Aye. And card and spin too," the shepherd answered, seeing that his daughter was too shy to answer herself.

"Good. Let the lassie come to me for two hours every afternoon and weave the plaid I am not yet strong enough to weave." And the witch nodded in the direction of the loom which stood under the little window. "The wool is spun and dyed and the sett is

one I saw in my dreams as I lay weak and ill on my bed and listened to the faint echoes of the music from the heart of Rubers Law."

The lassie looked at her father. Two hours a day when already so much of their own work had been neglected! And two hours a day alone with a witch!

"You helped me when I did not ask. You cannot refuse when I do. And the lassie will come to no harm, that I promise you."

"Let me do the weaving," the lassie said to her father. "I will get up before sunrise so that my own work is done."

So it was that each afternoon for two hours the lassie sat under the window in the tumbledown cottage on the flank of Rubers Law. First she set up the loom with varying shades and different colours as the witch instructed her: when the warp was closely spaced and taut she began to weave and the pattern was one she herself had never seen before and the colours different from those she knew, but from what lichens and roots the witch had obtained her dyes she did not know and dared not ask.

As the lassie wove, the witch spun and hummed a strange, haunting air that encouraged the steady rhythm of the flying shuttle. At first the witch called out the change of colour and the number of threads, but presently the lassie found herself humming the haunting air herself and finding that her fingers were touched with magic so that she repeated the sett faultlessly and without any further instructions from the witch.

A strange happiness filled her as she watched the chequered pattern of blues and green with its dividing lines of yellow growing day by day, and she knew this was a richer and more beautiful plaid than any she had ever woven before, or seen for sale in the market at Hawick, or observed flung over the shoulders of the wealthy farmers who went there to buy and sell their stock.

When at last the plaid was finished, the lassie cut the warp threads, knotted them into a fringe and brought the garment to the door for the witch to see.

"And where is the neuk?" the old woman asked, and the lassie sat down and sewed up one corner to form a pocket into which a lost lamb could snuggle and keep warm until its mother was found.

"Spread it out on the grass in front of my door. It will rain for three days and then the sun will shine and between them they will finish what you have begun. When the first frosts touch Rubers Law, come back here."

"Aye," the shepherd said, when he returned that evening and looked at the lowering skies to the east. "There is rain on the way, but as for sunshine . . . " and he shrugged his shoulders.

But the witch was right: whether it was simply because she was a witch or whether the Fairy People of Rubers Law had told her, the rain came and cleared after three days and the late autumn sun shone, and finally the lassie arose to find Rubers Law white with frost. Reluctantly – for not one word of thanks had the witch given her – she made her way back to the tumbledown cottage and there the plaid was, shrunk and firmed by the rain, smooth and softened by the sun, a garment such as would keep out the bitter winds and the driving rain and snow that swept the Lowland hills in winter.

"Take it," the witch said.

"Do you want my father to sell it at Hawick market for you?" the lassie asked, fingering the heavy wool plaid and comparing it with the old, worn, darned one her father wore.

The witch laughed.

"You came to my aid when others forgot me. You set up the loom and wove the plaid. Take it and do with it what you please." And she turned away as though deaf to the lassie's stammered thanks.

It was hers, the lassie thought, as she ran back home. It would sell for more money than they had ever possessed and her father could buy the two extra sheep on which he had set his heart, or perhaps even a cow, but just as she reached her cottage she saw her father approaching and once again she noticed how old and thin his plaid was and she thought of the chill, dark days of the coming winter.

"Father," she cried, "the Witch of Rubers Law taught me how to weave this plaid and she has given it to me to do with as I please: now I give it to you, so that you will not return cold and wet in the bitter days of winter."

"It is the finest weaving I have ever seen," the shepherd said, embracing his daughter. "This will keep me warm and dry when I am out on the hills and many a lost lamb, snuggling down in the neuk, will have cause to be grateful to you. I did not know there was such a sett, or such colours, or that you could weave in such a fashion."

"I did not know myself," the lassie admitted. "It was the witch who gave me the wool and guided my fingers. I doubt that I could weave such a plaid here at my mother's loom."

"Then I shall value it even more, and the first time I wear it will be tomorrow, when we go to the Kirk." There was, he knew, no reason to distrust the witch and her gift, but a wise man sought the blessing of the Kirk whenever possible.

Winter came suddenly and glad indeed was the shepherd of the fine plaid his daughter had woven for him.

"I shall take this old one with me to the market," he said, "and sell it for a few pence to help me buy two more sheep."

Whistling to his sheep dog, he took the old track that skirted Rubers Law and led to the river, but just as he glimpsed Teviot, white and ruffled by the driving wind, his collie halted and with her ears pricked, stared ahead, motionless.

"What is it, lass?" he asked.

But now he too could hear it – the sound of a woman weeping and, ever and again, the thin greeting of a bairn.

Snapping his fingers to the collie to follow at his heels, he strode on, and as he rounded a clump of fallen rocks he saw a woman crouched on a flat boulder, a bairn cradled in her arms. Backwards and forwards the woman rocked, the bitter wind tugging at her gown of grass green silk, blowing her long, pale hair now this way and now that, and all the time she wept softly, hopelessly and the bairn cried with the despair of a lost lamb.

"What ails you, good woman?" the shepherd asked, aware that his collie had drawn back and the hairs on her neck and back were standing stiff with fear.

"I am cold, so cold," the woman whispered. "And I have nothing except my gown of grass green silk in which to wrap my bairn." As she spoke, she looked up, and the shepherd, seeing the lost look in her eyes knew her at once for one of the Fairy People.

What she had done to be cast out of Rubers Law on a bitter winter morning like this he did not know, but he knew better than to ask. He could, he knew, hurry on and forget all about her, for everyone said the less you had to do with the Fairy People the better – they were mean and spiteful and delighted in bringing trouble to honest men and women. He would be wise, he thought, to let her own folk take her back to Rubers Law, or leave her and the bairn to perish in the cold.

A woman and a bairn? No. Even though they were Fairy People he could not abandon them, any more than he could have left the witch ill in her tumbledown cottage. How fortunate that he had brought his old, worn plaid to sell at the market at Hawick. Sell it? No, he would give it to this poor, cold creature. It had kept him warm many a long year, and his father before him.

He looked at the folded plaid under his arm and then fingered the fine thick garment the lassie had woven. There was a whole world of difference between the two, and the Fairy woman and her bairn were shivering in the biting wind.

Slowly he unfastened the plaid at his shoulder, carefully he placed it round the woman and watched as she put her bairn in the warm neuk and hugged it to her, and then, whistling to his dog, he strode off, flinging his old, worn plaid over his shoulder and wondering how he could explain to the lassie why he had given away her precious gift.

Given it away to one of the Fairy People, he thought, and not to a poor old widow woman who would have appreciated it.

Growing more and more concerned at the foolishness of what he had done, he wandered off the track – which was as well known to him as the back of his hand – and by the time he had retraced his steps and arrived at last at the market place at Hawick, the buying and selling was over, the farmers and shepherds gone and the pens empty – except for one, where a strange little fellow lounged, casting a casual eye from time to time on his six fine, fat sheep.

He had wanted to buy two sheep but he would be lucky if he could afford one of these, the shepherd thought; however, as there were none others to be had, he asked the stranger what he wanted for them.

"I'll take what you've got in your pocket," the little fellow answered.

"It isn't enough, and I must keep a little to buy what my lassie needs for our meals."

"I'll take half," the fellow said, helping himself from the coins in the shepherd's palm. "The six sheep are yours and good luck goes with them." He turned to go, halted, and looked over his shoulder. "There's some fine wool at yon stall there. I should buy it and get your lassie to weave you a new plaid for the one you're wearing won't keep warm man, or woman or greeting bairn."

When the shepherd and his collie arrived home with the six fine sheep, he told the lassie all that had happened, and looked at her anxiously, lest she should blame him for giving away so lightly the plaid she had woven for him. To his relief, she smiled happily.

"You did right, Father. From the first moment I started weaving at the loom in the witch's cottage, I knew it was the Fairy People who had taught her how to dye such colours and how to design such a sett and when the witch gave me the plaid, I think they were jealous that their secrets should be known to human beings.

"They could so easily have stolen it away. But they did not. They waited to see if you would give it back to one of them of your own accord. I think the sheep are a reward for your kindness."

With the wool her father had bought at the market, the lassie began to weave another plaid, and though she could almost remember the sett and could hum most of the strange, haunting air the witch had sung, and though her fingers were nimble and skilful, she knew there was now no magic in them.

The shepherd, however, did not seem to notice the difference and was well pleased with the finished plaid, which kept him warm and dry, and more than one lost lamb nestled in the neuk while he searched for its mother.

From that time he prospered amazingly. Each year he bought fresh stock and land and cultivated more ground, and when the younger son of a neighbouring farmer started walking home with them after the Sabbath service, he found that there was now more work than one man could manage, and other rooms were added to the cottage when the young man asked for the lassie's hand in marriage.

All their friends in Hawick and Teviotdale came to the wedding, and as the shepherd followed the bride and groom out of the Kirk, among the waiting, waving crowd he caught a glimpse of a woman in a gown of grass green silk with a plaid of unusual pattern over her shoulder, and beside her the strange little fellow who had sold him so cheaply the six, fine, fat sheep. When not far away, he spied the Witch of Rubers Law, nodding her head as though well contented, he smiled, knowing that good luck and happiness would go with him and his family all their lives.